Date: 1/17/20

LP FIC CARTLAND
Cartland, Barbara,
One minute to love

ONE MINUTE TO LOVE

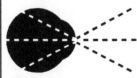

This Large Print Book carries the
Seal of Approval of N.A.V.H.

ONE MINUTE TO LOVE

BARBARA CARTLAND

THORNDIKE PRESS
A part of Gale, a Cengage Company

Farmington Hills, Mich • San Francisco • New York • Waterville, Maine
Meriden, Conn • Mason, Ohio • Chicago

LIBRARY OF CONGRESS CIP DATA ON FILE.
CATALOGUING IN PUBLICATION FOR THIS BOOK
IS AVAILABLE FROM THE LIBRARY OF CONGRESS

ISBN-13: 978-1-4328-6441-5 (hardcover alk. paper)

Published in 2019 by arrangement with Cartland Promotions

Printed in Mexico
2 3 4 5 6 7 23 22 21 20 19

"Everyone in the world falls in love at least once in their lifetime and it is always a life-changing experience that can never be forgotten."

Barbara Cartland

CHAPTER ONE
1887

Yolisa Warren rode out from the woods and across the Park towards the village.

She had a message from her father to leave at one of the cottages before she returned home for luncheon.

It was such a lovely day and she had enjoyed every moment of her ride under the shady trees.

The woods had always had a special attraction for her.

She had trotted slowly along the

mossy paths which twisted and turned under the silver elms.

She felt, as she did so, that the elves and fairies were whispering to her.

Because she was an only child she often told herself stories that she had a companion with her and he laughed at the same things as she did.

She rode out of the great iron gates and came in sight of the thatched cottages.

With their small flower beds in front of them they looked pretty and attractive. It was her mother who had always encouraged people in the village to grow flowers in their gardens.

She had herself created a large

Herb Garden at the back of Warren Court.

Yolisa now rode to the village shop which supplied almost everything that anyone could want in every station of life.

She dismounted.

There were some boys playing at the side of the road and she then called one of them over to hold her horse for her.

"You know that Achilles is always good with you, Jim."

Jim grinned.

"I loves them 'orses, Miss Yolisa," he said, "and when I'm big I'm goin' to be a jockey."

"Then you will have to learn to ride very well," Yolisa replied. "In the meantime you must try very hard to understand horses, as a horse goes better when he and his rider are compatible with each other."

Jim nodded, but she was not sure if he had followed what she was saying.

He was a clever little boy of eight and she had known him since he was born.

She went into the village shop and Mr. Hundell, when he saw her, hurried from where he was packing up a parcel.

"Good morning, Miss Yolisa," he then greeted her. "What can I do for you?"

"I have brought a letter from my father," Yolisa said, "and he wants me to thank you for the goods you sent to us yesterday. They are just what we wanted."

"That's what I likes to hear," Mr. Hundell smiled, "and I do hopes, Miss Yolisa, you're feelin' as good as you looks."

"Rather better," Yolisa laughed and went out into the sunshine.

She was just going to mount Achilles again when a young girl came running up to her. She was petite and good-looking in a rather tousled way.

"Oh, Miss Yolisa," she said, "please I've somethin' to ask you."

Yolisa stopped.

She knew only too well what was coming.

"It be Ben," the girl blurted out. "And 'e wants to marry me, but I can't make up my mind."

"You cannot expect me to do that for you," Yolisa replied.

" 'Tis just that I wants you to look into the future, Miss Yolisa, as you've done for me before and tell me if you thinks we'll be 'appy together."

Yolisa did not reply and the girl went on,

"There be someone else who be after me, but I be not sure of 'im either."

"It all comes," Yolisa said, "of being the prettiest girl in the village, Brenda."

Brenda giggled and looked coy.

"At least I've a choice, miss."

"That is true, Brenda, and I can understand that you are afraid of making the wrong decision."

"That's just what I be sayin', Miss Yolisa, and only you can tell me what to do."

"I cannot answer for your heart," Yolisa said, "but, knowing that Ben is a reliable man, I think you can at least consider him seriously."

"I see what you means, Miss Yolisa, and perhaps the other one be a bit flighty, so to speak."

"You have to decide for yourself what you want," Yolisa said. "But a flighty husband can have a roving eye and perhaps forget his family when he has other interests at heart."

Brenda thought for a moment.

She was undoubtedly a pretty girl. Rather on the plump side, but at the same time Yolisa was not surprised that the young men in the village found her enticing.

There was always someone proposing to her.

Yolisa had in fact had this conversation with her twice already.

She knew, with what her father called her *Third Eye,* that Brenda would settle down eventually and be a very good wife.

Now as Brenda did not speak, Yolisa added,

"What I should do if I was you, Brenda, is think it over carefully and before you do finally decide to marry one or the other, I should make quite certain that he will love you and you can always be sure of his protection and support."

"I think that I understands what you're sayin', Miss Yolisa," Brenda replied, "and that be Ben right enough."

"Then perhaps it had better be Ben," Yolisa said. "But if you are still worried, come to see me one evening when you finish work and I will tell the cards for you."

"Oh, I 'opes you'd do that, miss," Brenda cried. "Thank you, thank you! You knows as 'ow us all relies on you."

"That is what worries me!" Yolisa replied.

She knew, however, that Brenda was not listening and she turned towards Achilles.

Jim was patting his nose and talking to him in a low voice.

15

She felt that the boy was right in saying that when he was older he would work with horses.

"Thank you, Jim," she said, "and here is a penny to spend in the shop."

"Thank you, miss, thank you," Jim grinned, taking it eagerly.

At the same time he gave Achilles one last pat as Yolisa climbed onto the saddle.

Then, as Jim ran into the shop, she waved to him and turned Achilles round and rode back towards the gates of her home.

Ever since she was a child she had had a strange intuition about the future of other people.

Whatever she knew or told them invariably came true.

Some people thought that it was uncanny, but as her father frequently said to her,

"It is quite usual for people in Scotland to be fey and your mother was a Scot. You have inherited that from her and not from me."

"It often worries me," Yolisa confessed, "how they believe everything I tell them. I am so frightened that I might be wrong."

Her father looked at her for a moment before he replied,

"I don't think that that is quite true. When you are predicting the future for someone, I have the feeling that you are absolutely sure in your own mind that what you say will indeed come true."

Yolisa laughed.

"You are quite right, Papa. I am only covering my tracks in case anything really does go wrong."

"It does not seem to have done so so far," Sir John replied, "and you should wait until it happens before you start worrying."

"I am sure, Papa, that your advice is much better than mine," Yolisa said.

Equally she was aware that her 'predictions', as she always called them, came from a deep conviction that was so strange but compelling that she could not dispute it.

She was only three when it had first happened.

She had pointed to a man who had been taken on in the household by the butler to do odd jobs and said,

"Bad man, bad man, go 'way."

Her Nanny had been horrified.

"That is very rude of you, Yolisa," she had scolded her, "now say you are sorry to Jacob."

"Bad, bad," Yolisa had persisted.

She had then run away before Nanny could catch her.

Only a week later it was discovered that Jacob was systematically stealing things in the house.

He was caught when Sir John remembered where he had put a small amount of money and then found that half of it was gone.

Jacob was naturally instantly dismissed and after he had left quite a number of other items were found to be missing.

Yet no one had suspected him except for Yolisa.

After that there was incident after incident when something she pointed out or predicted was proved entirely correct.

As she grew older, in fact by the time she was in her teens, the servants regularly consulted her.

Of course the story of her powers quickly reached the village and surrounding towns.

It was impossible for anything concerning courtship to happen without her being consulted about it.

Sir John had to admit that he relied on her when he was engaging staff for the house and occasionally when he was negotiating with people he had some business contacts with.

To Yolisa it was a remarkable gift, as she insisted, from God, which she could not ignore.

"If I can help people, then I am very fortunate," she had said to her mother before she died. "I am just afraid, Mama, that I might tell them what was wrong and perhaps damage their lives."

"I am very sure, my dearest," Lady Warren replied, "that what you have is a gift from God. At the same time I quite understand that you are afraid of telling those who consult you what is not right. But you must trust your own intuition and pray you will never make a mistake."

"I always do that," Yolisa murmured.

"In that case I am sure that God will not fail you," Lady Warren answered.

Yolisa's mother had died in the middle of a very cold winter. She was weakened by a hacking cough which went to her lungs and eventually turned to pneumonia.

Yolisa was, at first, inconsolable.

She adored her mother in the same way she loved her father, but with her mother she had a special affinity.

It was so close that, when her mother died, she felt that half of herself had gone with her.

Gradually she came to realise that her mother was still there to guide her and help her as she always had done in the past.

Yolisa did not talk to anyone about it because they would not have understood.

However she was vividly conscious of her mother's presence whenever she was undertaking a task that was too big or difficult for her.

Now as Yolisa rode back home, she was thinking how fond her mother had been of everyone who lived in the village.

They had loved her and indeed five years after her death her grave always had little bunches of flowers on it from those who lived in the nearby cottages.

At times Yolisa had seen the first

fruits arranged on their leaves beneath the tombstone.

"They have never forgotten
Mama," she said once to her father.

"How could they?" Sir John had
replied. "Just as she lives in your
memory and mine, she lives in
theirs."

It was what Yolisa thought herself
and because she knew how much
her father missed his wife she
would put her arms round him and
kiss his cheek.

"I am so lucky to have you, Papa,"
she would sigh, "and that, I know,
is what Mama would want."

"I can say the same, my dearest,"
her father replied. "And she would
want us to carry on making the
house and the garden as beautiful

as it was when she was here and, of course, looking after other people as she did."

"Which you do magnificently Papa," Yolisa smiled. "Colin was telling me yesterday how you promised to help him set up his own business. That was very kind of you."

"He is a good boy," Sir John said, "and his father and mother have lived on this estate for over fifty years."

"Then they are certainly one of us," Yolisa laughed and kissed her father again.

Now, as she rode nearer the house, she thought how lovely it was.

It had been built in Tudor times,

a black and white house with diamond-paned casement windows.

Over centuries it had been enlarged as the family increased in size and yet it still looked as it had originally and was listed as one of the best preserved Tudor mansions in the country.

There was a stream running below it where swam a variety of ducks, some of them quite rare.

They were Sir John's special hobby and enthusiasts came from all over the country to admire them and consult him on their breeding.

Now, as it was spring, the ducks were followed by their ducklings.

They made a very pretty picture as they moved over the water that was sparkling in the bright sun-shine.

Sir John had always said that it was entirely due to the stream that Yolisa's eyes were of the same soft green flecked with gold.

Her skin was very white and she had hair which was such pale gold that it was the colour of the dawn.

Sir John had often said to his wife, "Yolisa is beautiful, but hers is a beauty so different from what I have ever seen before that I am not certain how to describe it."

"There is no need to do so," Lady Warren replied. "Yolisa comes from the woods and the flowers and how could one possibly describe them in one word?"

Sir John laughed.

"That is very true and it is to be expected, I would suppose, that your daughter would be completely different from any other child."

At first, after their marriage, it had been a great sadness to him that they could not have any more children.

But as Yolisa grew older, he began to realise that it would be greedy to ask for anything more.

He had a daughter who was so original and in her own way so lovely that she was definitely unique.

It had been a surprise to him that she should have the gift of prediction.

Many people exclaimed about it almost critically, as if it was grossly unfair that Yolisa should be so different from them.

"I am a very fortunate man," Sir John often said to his contemporaries and they had not argued with him.

When Yolisa then reached the house, she did not dismount but rode to the stable yard.

There were quite a number of horses there, because her father was a brilliant rider and he could never resist buying a horse if it was in any way exceptional.

There was, therefore, in the stables always a large choice of mounts for Yolisa to select one from.

But Achilles was her definite favourite.

As she reached the stables, the Head Groom came hurrying towards her.

"Achilles gave me such a wonderful ride, Jarvis," she said, "and we jumped all the hedges with at least six inches to spare."

"I thinks you'd be a-doin' that, Miss Yolisa," Jarvis replied. "And I be waitin' for you to try the new 'orse, Robin, as Sir John calls 'im."

"I will try him tomorrow," Yolisa promised.

She had already heard a great deal about the new horse from her father.

He had had a name before he arrived, but they had made a pact between them.

It was that all the new horses

would be called after birds or insects that lived on the estate and it was getting hard to think of new names.

Yolisa thought that 'Robin' was a good name for this particular horse because he was a deep dark brown in colour.

She patted Achilles before he was taken away and then walked back to the house.

As she went in through the front door, the elderly butler greeted her with a smile,

"Sir John's in the study, Miss Yolisa, if you should want him."

"Then I will go at once to see him and warn him that it is nearly luncheontime, Yolisa replied.

She knew that, if her father was

busy with the book he was writing, he would have no idea of the time.

It was a history of his ancestors and a very detailed account not only of the battles they had fought in but of the houses they had owned.

The family had spread out over the country since Norman times when the very first Warren had arrived with William the Conqueror.

Although Sir John had been working on this book for nearly two years, he had not yet finished it.

He had, in fact, turned up old manuscripts in every part of England and Yolisa had teased him.

"When the book is finished, Papa," she said, "it will be too large to go on any ordinary shelf!"

It was not the first book that Sir John had written, but it was one that he found the most absorbing.

Yolisa knew now as she opened the study door that he had forgotten the time and was totally immersed in his writing.

She walked across the room to where he was sitting at the writing table in front of the window.

She put one hand on his shoulder and pressed her cheek against his.

"Where have you got to now, Papa?" she enquired. "Have I been born yet?"

"Not quite, my dearest," Sir John replied. "But you will certainly appear in the next chapter."

"Which must be the last," Yolisa said. "Otherwise the book will need three men and a boy to carry it!"

Sir John chuckled.

"It has certainly become rather a tome. At the same time I am convinced that you will find it interesting as well as informative."

"I have indeed read most of it already and found it enchanting," Yolisa replied. "But now, Papa, it is time for luncheon."

"Luncheon?" Sir John asked vaguely, as if he had never heard of it. "I thought we had eaten it already."

"If you are not hungry, I am," Yolisa said. "So, please, Papa, put down your pen. I will be ready for you in just two minutes after I have washed my hands."

She kissed him again affectionately and ran from the room.

Sir John looked after her with a little sigh. He often wondered what would happen to his daughter.

Would there ever be a man who he would think was good enough to marry her?

He had lived a very interesting life himself and had mixed with a great variety of people.

He was well aware that Yolisa was different from other girls of her age.

So different he was afraid that she would be hurt or upset by what went on outside her home.

He could not imagine any man he had met so far to be in any way suitable for his lovely daughter.

He was afraid that she might marry someone who would not

understand her and he would make her unhappy because he was incapable of appreciating how unusual and original she was.

Sir John walked from his study towards the dining room.

He was thinking as he did so that, now spring was here, he ought to take Yolisa to London for the Season.

She was eighteen and should be presented at Court as a *debutante.*

It was something he ought to have arranged before now, but, because he had been so happy to have her with him, he had thought only of their horses, the estate and his book.

He had just reached the dining room when Yolisa came hurrying after him.

"I have had such a wonderful ride on Achilles this morning, Papa, but I had to promise Jarvis that I would ride Robin tomorrow."

"As you know, I rode him before breakfast," Sir John replied, "and I think you will be surprised how easy he is to ride. Equally he is one of the most outstanding horses I have ever ridden."

"Which is high praise indeed!" Yolisa laughed.

They sat down in the very attractive dining room with its beamed ceiling and large Medieval fireplace.

It was a room which seemed to be part of history and Yolisa had often thought that her ancestors were with them at the long polished refectory table, which had been in the room ever since the house was built.

Because Sir John was a wealthy man, the food was delicious and they were waited on by a butler and two footmen.

"What are we going to do this afternoon?" Yolisa asked as they finished the last course.

Her father did not answer and she went on,

"You are not going back to your book, Papa. You know that Mama said it was bad for you to work for too long, especially when the sun is shining brightly. Let's go some-where new and exciting."

"I do think, my dearest," Sir John

said, "what we actually ought to do is to plan a visit to London."

"To London!" she exclaimed in astonishment. "But why?"

"Because I am depriving you of meeting people of your own age. You should be attending balls and parties, in fact becoming a Social *debutante.* Your mother would certainly have expected it to happen were she to be still with us."

Yolisa stared at him.

Her father had been so desperately unhappy when her mother died and she had therefore been so busy trying, in her own way, to fill the gap in his life that she had not thought of herself.

She had dispensed with her Governess ten months ago. The last one who had been with her for some years had retired and her place had not been filled.

Yolisa had told her father that he was a lesson in himself and so was the library with its thousands of books on practically every subject known to man.

Because it suited Sir John and certainly eased his loneliness, he agreed to everything Yolisa had suggested.

But now he knew that the time had come when he must stop thinking about himself.

"We are going to London," he said firmly, "and we will open the house up in Berkeley Square. Your cousin to whom I lent it, left, now I think about it, over three months ago."

"Perhaps it will be really exciting to go to London," Yolisa said slowly, "but I am – very happy here, Papa."

"You have to meet new people," her father insisted, "and not just the same neighbours we see here over and over again."

"But we love them and they in turn love us," Yolisa answered. "To London people we shall just be strangers."

"Not quite as strange as all that," he argued. "Your mother and I made many friends there who I know will be only too delighted to meet you. I will write to them before we arrive."

Yolisa did not say anything, but he knew that she was listening and went on,

"We will start giving luncheon and dinner parties which will be reciprocated by your having invitations to go to their houses."

"I shall have to buy so many new clothes," Yolisa sighed, "and start an entirely new life."

She was almost talking to herself as she continued,

"I shall miss all the horses, the ducks on the stream and, of course, the garden. Oh, Papa, are we doing a wise thing in going to London?"

"It is most certainly wise for you, my dearest," Sir John declared.

As he spoke, the door of the dining room opened and the butler announced,

"Lord Langford, Sir John."

Sir John looked up in astonishment.

"Harold!" he exclaimed. "I was not expecting to see you."

"Am I too late for something to eat?" the newcomer asked. "I have been longer getting here than I expected and quite frankly I am starving!"

As he was speaking Lord Langford walked towards Sir John and it was easy to see the resemblance between the two brothers.

Sir John was the elder of the two by three years, but Lord Langford looked young for his age.

Yolisa jumped up from her chair at once and ran to his side.

"It's so lovely to see you, Uncle Harold," she said, "but we thought you were abroad."

"I was indeed until a few days ago," Lord Langford replied. "Now I am here back in England to find that it has not altered much since I have been away."

Sir John laughed.

"What did you expect? A revolution?"

Lord Langford sat down at the table.

Footmen hurriedly laid knives and forks in front of him and the butler poured out a glass of wine.

Lord Langford drank a little of it.

"I needed that," he said. "Now do tell me how you are, John. I can see that Yolisa is looking more beautiful than ever and has grown a bit since I last saw her."

"I have grown a bit older," Yolisa said, "and Papa has just been saying that I have to go to London and be a *debutante.*"

"Good Heavens!" Lord Langford exclaimed. "I did think that you were one already."

"Only here in our County," Yolisa replied. "So according to Papa I must do the right thing and enter the Social world."

"That might be a big mistake," Lord Langford said. "I have always thought of you being unique here in your little Kingdom. I must tell you that your prediction about the man I brought with me the last time I came here was absolutely right. In fact he was not only everything you said he was, but he was killed in a very unpleasant manner by one of the people he had deceived."

Yolisa drew in her breath.

"I saw that too," she murmured, "but I did not like to tell you exactly what would happen."

"You told me enough to make me sure that he was a villain, which he most undoubtedly was," Lord Langford replied, "and he received his just desserts."

Yolisa gave a little shiver.

"I was sure of that the moment I met him," she said in a low voice.

"I ought to apologise," her uncle sighed, "for ever doubting that you were right. But at least you made me suspicious and, when everything you predicted came true, I realised that I had been extremely stupid in ever doubting you."

"I am not really surprised that you did," Sir John chimed into the conversation. "I thought at the time that Yolisa was laying it on rather thick, but apparently she was right."

"Completely and absolutely," Lord Langford said, "and next time, Yolisa, I want the whole truth."

"That is what I usually do give you," she replied, "but this was so horrifying that I really could not believe it myself."

"I quite understand you feeling like that," her uncle said. "At the same time there was so much at stake that the more I understood the better."

As he spoke, a footman offered him some food.

When Lord Langford was helping himself, Sir John suggested,

"Now let's talk of more cheerful things and tell me why you are back in England."

"I had to see the Prime Minister," Lord Langford replied, "and, of course, the Secretary of State for Foreign Affairs, who, as you know is the Earl of Iddesleigh."

"Yes, of course," Sir John nodded.

"You will not in the least be surprised to hear that he has another mission for me and one which appears to be a very difficult one."

Sir John chuckled.

"You know as well as I do,

Harold, that you enjoy every moment of the intrigue. While the 'powers that be' are extremely grateful."

Because of his extensive and distinguished work in the Diplomatic Service, Lord Langford had been made a Peer of the Realm.

For his title he had chosen the name of the house that he had inherited from his wife. A considerable heiress, she had died over ten years ago and he had never married again.

This was because, Yolisa thought, he enjoyed his life of continual movement and activity.

Whenever there was a difficult Diplomatic problem and whenever Queen Victoria required special information that was not obtainable from the usual channels, the Prime Minister sent for Lord Langford.

He invariably succeeded in his many missions and those who served with him said that he had a magic quality all of his own.

Whether it was unearthing the information required or distinguishing the reliable reports from the unreliable, he succeeded where other Diplomats failed.

Lord Langford's glass was replenished and he was eating his luncheon quickly.

Because the servants were present in the room, Sir John thought it somewhat unwise to ask too many intimate questions.

So he told his brother what he had been doing and about the horses he had bought and the improvements he had made on the estate and in the local villages.

Lord Langford was clearly listening carefully to his brother's dissertation.

But at the same time Yolisa had the idea that he was looking mostly at her, almost as if he was scrutinising her.

Finally Lord Langford finished his luncheon with a large helping of cream cheese and then he was left with a cup of coffee and a full glass of port.

The servants then withdrew discreetly to the pantry.

When the door into the pantry

closed, Sir John said,

"Now, Harold, please tell us the real reason you are here."

There was a pause before Lord Langford replied to his brother,

"I have come to you straight from No. 10 Downing Street. I have been given a mission which I think will be very difficult to handle. But the Prime Minister said that he relies on me and he cannot think of anyone else to take my place."

"The usual compliment then," Sir John remarked. "I think you are brilliant, Harold, in what you do and I am thankful that our father sent me into the family Regiment, while you went into the Diplomatic Service."

"I think the truth was," Lord

Langford replied, "I did rather better than you at Oxford University and had a good aptitude for foreign languages! Otherwise I would be doing exactly the same as you."

As Yolisa thought that he was almost disparaging her father, she said quickly,

"Papa has nearly finished his second book and you do know, Uncle Harold, that you will have to write one yourself eventually."

Lord Langford held up his hands.

"God forbid!" he exclaimed. "If I did write one, it would be extremely libellous and I should doubtless end up behind bars!"

"Then you had better keep to what you really do well," his brother volunteered.

"That is just what I intend to do," Lord Langford replied, "but I need your help."

"My help?" Sir John enquired. "How can I possibly help you?"

"It's quite simple," Lord Langford responded. "I want you to lend me Yolisa."

There was silence.

Then Sir John quizzed him,

"What do you mean, lend you Yolisa?"

Lord Langford leaned back comfortably in his high chair.

"The mission I have been given," he said, "will take me to one of the smaller countries in the Balkans. It is, the Prime Minister believes, in danger of being taken over by the Russians."

Sir John raised his eyebrows but did not speak and Lord Langford went on,

"The Czar is like all his predecessors, determined to expand Russia by taking over all the smaller countries in the Balkans that he can."

"As a number of them have an English Queen and therefore our protection," Sir John said, "I should have thought that they were safe enough."

"That is what Her Majesty feels," Lord Langford answered, "but some of them are insecure and the Russians are infiltrating the Balkans wherever they possibly can in a most shameless manner and from 'under the counter', so to speak, are gaining control."

"So I would suppose that it is something we might have anticipated," Sir John said, "after Bismarck wanted so much of Germany."

"It is something that Her Majesty wishes to stop or rather prevent," Lord Langford said sharply. "This mission which I have undertaken concerns one small Principality, but like many others it would be in itself a dangerous 'hole in the wall' if Russia took it under her control."

"You really think you can prevent that happening?" Sir John asked.

Lord Langford shrugged his shoulders.

"I can but try, but in all these problems it is always difficult to know what is happening underground and when one does discover anything useful it is often too late."

"I can understand that," Sir John agreed.

"That is why I want Yolisa," Lord Langford said again.

"You cannot be serious!" her father ejaculated.

"I am very serious," his brother replied. "To know what is about to occur is to be forearmed. If I wait until it does happen, then, as I have just said, it is too late. What is done is done and there is not a thing one can do but accept it."

"I understand what you are saying," Sir John said, "but I don't want my Yolisa to be mixed up in your highly dramatic, intriguing, but undoubtedly dangerous life."

"She will not run into danger, I promise you that. She will just be able to identify for me the people I can trust and those who I cannot. Quite frankly I know enough about this Balkan country to realise it will be impossible for me to be absolutely sure of the truth as things stand at the moment."

There was a complete silence until he went on,

"It is just a question of time. If we wait too long, Russia will step in with armed force and it will be too late to prevent her doing so without going to war."

He paused to gaze at Yolisa before he continued,

"If however I know what is likely to happen before it does happen, then I have a chance, only a small one I grant you, of preventing a disaster that both the Queen and the Prime Minister fear at the present time is very likely to happen."

"I can understand your reasoning," Sir John said. "But very candidly, Harold, I don't want my daughter to be mixed up in all that sort of cloak and dagger drama at her age."

"I can appreciate your saying that about an ordinary young girl of eighteen," Lord Langford said, "but Yolisa is different. You know just as well as I do that she has this amazing gift of knowing if a man is guilty or not guilty by just meeting him."

He paused, but, as his brother did

not say anything, he continued,

"She can predict the future which invariably comes true and she has the advantage over every other clairvoyant or whatever you may want to call them, of looking young, innocent and very beautiful."

"I still think," Sir John said, "she is far too young. She should be thinking of the compliments she will receive from the young men who will dance with her, rather than be occupied with sinister men in dark streets and predicting who intends to murder who."

Lord Langford spread out his hands.

"Of course you are right, John, nobody can dispute that. But, if I don't have Yolisa, how am I to carry out the instructions of Her Majesty and the Prime Minister? They are both desperate as to where they can turn to for help and save a Prince from losing his Throne in the Balkans to the traitorous Russians."

There was silence.

Then Sir John felt Yolisa's hand slip into his.

"I think, Papa," she said quietly, "that Mama would want us to help Uncle Harold with his problems. In fact I know that she would."

CHAPTER TWO

Lord Langford said that he must return to London the following day and would take Yolisa with him.

When he suggested it, she gave a scream of horror.

"But Uncle Harold, I have to pack and I don't know what clothes I am to take with me or if I have everything I shall need."

"I shall buy you what you want in London," Lord Langford replied. "Just pack a few of your prettiest dresses and evening gowns."

Yolisa wanted to ask him many questions, but he was obviously not inclined to answer them, so she stayed silent.

At the same time she was exceedingly curious.

However, she had so much to do in choosing what clothes she wanted the maids to pack and there was really no time to think about anything else.

Fortunately she had several pretty summer dresses and three passable evening gowns.

She thought sadly that they were scarcely what her uncle would expect her to wear if they were to be going to fashionable parties or Receptions.

Wherever they went she was sure

that he would be acclaimed as an influential representative of Great Britain and would be fêted by his foreign hosts.

It was all very exciting.

But when Yolisa went to bed, she found it difficult to sleep.

She was trying to guess what lay ahead of her and she was also a little afraid in case she should make a mess of it.

However, it was very flattering to think that her uncle relied on her so much, although it was quite different from predicting the future for a village girl.

She was nervous of being confronted by foreigners on whom the future of a country rested.

She was aware too that her father

was uneasy about what she was to do and naturally he wanted her to stay at home.

When she was alone with him, she said,

"Please don't worry about me, Papa. If things are too difficult I will persuade Uncle Harold to send me back to you."

"Promise me that you will do so," Sir John replied, "because quite frankly, my dearest, I do not at all like your undertaking this journey and I am afraid that it may end in disaster."

Yolisa laughed.

"I cannot believe that it will be as bad as that, Papa, and that I shall come home in disgrace."

"If you do," her father replied, "I

will be waiting here to welcome you with open arms."

She kissed him.

But she was wishing that by helping her uncle she did not have to upset her father.

They set off for London, driving first to the nearest Railway Station.

They had a special compartment to themselves after being locked in by an efficient Station Master.

He was obviously impressed by Lord Langford and stood bowing on the platform as the train steamed out of the Station.

Only when they were well on their way did Lord Langford speak up,

"I want to talk to you, Yolisa, and, as this is a safe place to do so, come and sit beside me."

Yolisa thought that it was strange for him to use the word 'safe'.

But she did not ask him any questions and crossed over to his side of the compartment.

She noticed that her uncle looked at the door which led into the corridor, as if he suspected that someone might be outside.

Then he said,

"Now I have so much to tell you and I want you to listen to it all carefully and intelligently as it is extremely important."

"I am listening, Uncle Harold," Yolisa answered.

There was then a little pause as if her uncle was choosing his words.

"I don't know," he began, "whether you remember last year

that there was a great commotion in Bulgaria."

"I think I remember Papa saying something about the Russians behaving very badly," Yolisa replied, "but I was not particularly interested."

"Well, you have to be interested now because what happened then deeply concerns you."

Yolisa opened her eyes wide in surprise.

"As I expect you know," Lord Langford went on, "after Bismarck unified most of Germany and made it into a vast Empire, the Russians became determined to extend their own authority in Europe."

"I am aware of that," Yolisa murmured.

"Czar Alexander III," Lord Langford continued, "is a very dangerous man. He has been furious ever since the Russian-Turkish War that his country failed to gain control of the Bosporus and the Dardanelles and to dominate the Balkans."

He stopped for a moment to say in a very positive voice,

"What he wanted, of course, was direct access to the Mediterranean."

Yolisa then made a little sound to indicate that she was following him and her uncle carried on,

"Bulgaria, at the Congress of Berlin, was split into two sections. And the Czar was determined to control the half that was ruled by his first cousin, Prince Alexander of Battenburg."

"Now I do remember something about that!" Yolisa exclaimed.

"The Russians could not afford another open war," her uncle said, "so the Czar waged a secret underground campaign by stirring up trouble with all the established Regimes."

"How did he do that?" Yolisa asked.

"In a multitude of different ways," Lord Langford replied. "But I need not go into that now. Sufficient to say that Russian Embassy Officials even paid crowds to start riots."

"Which was cheating!" Yolisa cried.

"The Czar tried dozens of different plots," her uncle said, "but he was still not successful as Prince Alexander of Battenburg refused to act as a Russian puppet. What the Czar wanted was to dispose of him and then unite the two countries under a Russian Prince."

"So what happened?" Yolisa enquired.

"Russian secret agents began to stir up a mutiny in the Bulgarian Army. They kidnapped Prince Alexander and forced him to abdicate at pistol point. He was taken by sea and deposited in the Russian port of Reni."

"How appalling!" she exclaimed. "What happened then?"

"There was a tremendous outcry in Europe and Her Majesty Queen Victoria then said that the behaviour of the Russians was 'without parallel in modern history'. In fact, there was such an outcry that the Russians were obliged to return the Prince to Bulgaria."

"So he went back," Yolisa said.

"He went back, but he was so disillusioned by the treachery of the Bulgarian Army that two weeks later he surrendered his Throne."

"Oh no! That is a wrong ending to the story!"

"Exactly what I thought myself," her uncle replied, "and, of course, the Czar was elated and believed that he had won."

"As he had."

"It was not as simple as that. The new Regime in Bulgaria is led by a staunch patriot, who is just as hostile to Russia as the Prince had been. In fact I am told secretly that Russian agents are now concentrating on murdering the new Ruler."

"Just how can they behave so shockingly?" Yolisa asked. "Surely someone must stop them."

"The only country that Russia is at all frightened of," Lord Langford said, "is Great Britain. That is why we have to prevent them from expanding, as they are trying to do, all over Asia as well, adding thousands of square miles to the Russian Empire on a regular basis."

"Are we managing to prevent them so far?" Yolisa asked.

"We are doing our very best, but, what the Prime Minister and Her Majesty consider at the moment more important than anything else, is that they should not gain access to the Mediterranean."

"How can we stop them from doing that?" Yolisa wanted to know.

"That is exactly what I am going to tell you," Lord Langford said, "and now this is where you come into the picture."

"Me?"

"Yes, you."

Lord Langford glanced again at the door into the corridor.

It was closed and there was no one to be seen and yet Yolisa knew that he was afraid of being overheard.

Keeping his voice low, he continued,

"As everyone is aware, Her Majesty the Queen has supplied a number of English Royal brides to the countries which are holding out against the Russian menace."

Yolisa smiled.

"I have been told that Her Majesty is called 'the Matchmaker of Europe'."

"That is true," her uncle answered, "and, when they can fly the Union Jack beside their own flag, these small Principalities feel secure and then are not so afraid of the Russians as they would be otherwise. But now there is one particular small Kingdom which is, at this very moment, in grave danger."

"Why is that, Uncle Harold?"

"Because," her uncle replied, "it is impossible for Her Majesty to give Prince Nikos of Kavalla all that he requires."

"Which is?"

"A wife," her uncle answered.

He saw that she was looking at him questioningly and he explained,

"Kavalla is a small State bordered on one side by Macedonia, on the other by Thrace and on the South by the Aegean Sea. If the Russians can gain control of it, they will gain access to the Aegean and the Mediterranean."

"Now I can understand," Yolisa said, "why Prince Nikos requires an English wife."

"It is the only safeguard that will defend him from being overrun, as most of his neighbours have been, by the Russians."

"Then why does Her Majesty not provide him with an English Princess?" Yolisa enquired.

"The answer is quite simple. The Queen has, for the moment, run out of relations of marriageable age. She has one in mind who would suit Prince Nikos perfectly, but she is only fifteen."

"That is certainly too young to be married," Yolisa concurred.

"It is something that might happen in the East, but not in the West. But the Prime Minister and I have thought up somewhat complicated means by which we can keep the Russians at arm's length until Prince Nikos's bride-to-be is old enough to take her place beside him on the Throne of Kavalla."

"That sounds most intriguing," Yolisa said. "Do tell me what you have planned to do."

"It is rather involved, so listen intently."

"I will, I promise you," Yolisa answered.

At the same time she was wondering how she came into this plot.

If, as her uncle had said, he required her *Third Eye* to warn him of who was threatening the Prince, it should not be too difficult.

Obviously any Russians actually in Kavalla would be suspect without him having to point them out.

"Now what we have to do," he was saying in a very low tone, "is to keep those Russians from interfering in Kavalla until his chosen bride has her sixteenth birthday. It is young for anyone to be married, but if the engagement is announced and then the Wedding preparations take many months, which is quite usual, then the bride will be nearly seventeen."

He smiled before he finished almost triumphantly,

"Old enough for it to be considered quite in order for her to sit on the Throne of Kavalla."

"Perhaps she will find it rather frightening," Yolisa suggested.

"I think that any young woman," Lord Langford answered, "would feel that it was like a Fairytale and I can assure you that Prince Nikos is very much just what one expects of a Prince Charming."

Yolisa laughed.

"I see, Uncle Harold, that you have it all tidied up. So why do you want me?"

"That is what I am now going to tell you," her uncle answered.

There was a silence as if he was feeling for his words.

Then he said,

"Her Majesty and the Marquis of Salisbury are very afraid that, if Russia knows that we are merely waiting for the Princess in question to grow older, they will accelerate the trouble they are making and try to push Prince Nikos off the Throne as quickly as possible."

Yolisa gave a little cry.

"I never thought of that! Of

course it is obvious that is what they will do."

"That is what we thought, which is why we have a plan to deceive them and so keep them afraid of offending Great Britain."

Because this scenario sounded so intriguing, Yolisa moved a little nearer to him.

"What is absolutely essential," Lord Langford said, "is that they should have no idea who the Princess is that Her Majesty has in mind. If they know that, they will realise how young she is and that they must go into action immediately to remove the Prince from the Throne."

"That is obvious," Yolisa murmured.

"So we have to side-track them into thinking that there is already a suitable Princess. And so that, my dear niece, is why you are coming with me to Kavalla."

Yolisa looked at him in surprise.

"I really — don't understand," she muttered.

"You must realise," Lord Langford replied, "that, if we introduce you as a Princess and even if you played the part of one very convincingly, it would still be quite easy for them to discover that no such person exists. We could then easily have made things much worse than they are already."

"But of course I could not pretend to be a Princess," Yolisa said. "And, however impressive a name you gave me, it would not be in the *Almanach de Gotha.*"

"That is exactly what we thought," Lord Langford replied.

"So if you cannot produce a false Princess," Yolisa said, "and it certainly cannot be me, what can you do?"

"We are going to be a little more subtle," her uncle continued. "You are coming with me to Kavalla as my niece, Lady Yolisa Ford."

"Well, no one will believe I am going to marry the Prince," Yolisa laughed.

"That is just what they have to do."

Yolisa stared at him.

"It's impossible."

"Not if you play the part I plan

for you," he replied, "so listen to what I have to say."

"I am listening, of course, I am listening," Yolisa said slightly irritably.

She was, however, entirely bewildered and could not imagine in any way what her uncle was trying to tell her.

"What you will do," Lord Langford said slowly, "is come to Kavalla, pretending to be only my niece in order to meet Prince Nikos and make up your mind as to whether or not you will be his wife. Because you are being difficult about this, the British Government is deliberately trying to deceive everyone into thinking that you are just an ordinary young Society beauty."

Yolisa gave a little laugh and he went on,

"You are paying a visit to Kavalla with me and so people who meet us will only think that you are charming and very beautiful and it is not surprising that the Prince is delighted to make your acquaintance."

"I still don't understand," Yolisa murmured.

"What those Russian spies, and there are a great number of them, will notice," Lord Langford said, "is that you are treated with unusual respect by me and the rest of your party."

He paused a moment before resuming,

"In fact they will suspect that the two people who will be accompanying us on our journey are really a Lady-in-Waiting and a Palace Official who would, under other circumstances, have the position of your Comptroller."

Yolisa was staring at him in astonishment, but she did not speak and he continued,

"They, as well as I, will be rather over-polite to a young girl who is supposedly only Lady Yolisa Ford, but they will occasionally stumble over addressing you as 'my Lady', as if about to say 'Your Royal Highness'."

He then gave a little laugh.

"The Russians will note all this and they will be convinced that the

Queen is providing Prince Nikos with what they fear is a British Royal bride, who does not yet wish her identity to be revealed."

Lord Langford eventually finished speaking.

Yolisa sat staring at him.

And then she said,

"It's impossible, Uncle! How could I play a part that is so difficult? And suppose they discover who I really am?"

"There is no reason why they should," he assured her. "They will be bewildered at first, then in their crafty minds they will become certain that something is going on and they have been clever enough to become aware of it."

"I am beginning to understand

now what you are trying to do," Yolisa said. "The drawback is that we may fail. Then, as the Prince will have to wait for so long for the real Princess, the Russians may then strike quickly and somehow spirit him away."

"We shall do everything in our power to prevent that," Lord Langford said. "Equally it will be difficult for them to prove that you are not a Princess incognito."

He gave a little laugh again before he added,

"The Russians always suspect the worst. I assure you that it will not be difficult to make them suspicious as soon as we arrive. Then all we have to do is to keep them at bay until the Prince's engagement is announced and the formalities can easily take considerably longer than is the usual case."

"I can see your plan much better now," Yolisa said, "and I think it is very clever of you, Uncle Harold. But I am beginning to feel nervous about my own part in the drama."

"I think what you have to do, my dearest, is simply to use your intuition. Your *Third Eye* will tell you who our enemies are before they can do us any damage."

"I hope I shall recognise them," Yolisa sighed. "At the same time I am frightened that, if I fail to convince them that I am in fact this mythical Princess, the Prince will lose his Throne."

"He could easily do that," Lord

Langford agreed, "but I know that both Her Majesty and the Prime Minister have spent many sleepless nights wondering what they can do and have come to the conclusion that this is the only possible way of gaining time until the real Princess grows a little older."

Unexpectedly Yolisa laughed.

"It's far too much like fiction," she said, "to be true. Not a Fairytale, but one of those stories one reads in books where one is never sure whether good or bad will triumph in the end."

"In this story the good *has* to win," Lord Langford said firmly. "The Russians are doing quite enough damage already in Europe and in Asia. Everyone knows it would be a real disaster if they could gain the entry they need so desperately into the Aegean Sea."

"All I can say," Yolisa said in a very small voice, "is that I am — very frightened of failing you."

Her uncle put his arm round her.

"I can think of no one else I would trust with such a very difficult mission. To be frank with you, my dearest, I considered quite a number of women, but knew that I could not trust them."

"Why not?" Yolisa asked.

"Because women talk," he replied, "and one word to leak out about our scheme would not only be a disaster from the Prince's point of view but it would make us the laughing stock of Europe."

"I will be very careful," Yolisa promised, "and, of course, I will speak to no one."

"The only time that you can talk with ease," Lord Langford said, "is when you are in the open air. Talk in the garden, talk when you are riding over the open fields, but remember that inside the Palace the Russians have ears even though you don't see them."

"The very idea of it is — terrifying," Yolisa said.

"That is what I always feel myself whenever I am anywhere where there might be a Russian. The advice I give you is what I follow myself and that is to trust no one."

"I will try to do what you say," Yolisa said. "At the same time you must tell me who knows the truth."

"There will be two people who will travel with us. They will come from the British Foreign Office and they both have a history of being exceedingly useful in the most unlikely diplomatic circumstances."

Her uncle smiled at her before he went on,

"We will never know their real names because that would be a mistake, but while they travel with us, the lady will be called Lady Saville and she will be suspected of being your Lady-in-Waiting while Colonel Bentley, an ex-Army Officer, would make an excellent Comptroller in any Royal Household."

"So what does he do when he is

not disguised as someone else?" Yolisa asked.

"That sort of question is totally forbidden. You will think of him and speak to him as Colonel and I can assure you, if the Russians look him up, they will find out that he was in command for some years of a distinguished British Regiment."

Yolisa laughed.

"I can see you have thought of every detail."

"We have to," her uncle replied. "I should not be so frank with you, Yolisa, if it was not essential that you know how to play your part and not make any dreadful mistakes."

"Well, I am very thankful for one thing, that I don't have to pretend to be your niece," she said.

"With a little reserve and less familiarity than you give me at the moment," Lord Langford answered.

Yolisa laughed again.

But she did realise that her uncle was being very serious.

Then suddenly she gave a little cry,

"I just thought of something. I cannot believe that the Russians will think I am really an important Princess when my clothes will most certainly not be grand enough for Royal occasions."

"I have thought of that already," Lord Langford replied. "The best dressmakers in London will be waiting for you when we arrive at my house in Belgrave Square. They have been told that you require your dresses because we are going to visit a number of European countries when we leave England."

Yolisa drew in her breath.

"Then you must tell me exactly what you have told the dressmakers otherwise I shall get into a muddle and say the wrong thing."

"You must talk as little as possible," he replied, "and the dresses will have to be ready for us to leave the day after tomorrow."

Yolisa wondered if this was in any way possible, but her uncle went on,

"What we are also taking with us to impress the Russians are my wife's jewels."

Yolisa looked at him in surprise and Lord Langford said,

"They have always been described as magnificent, and, of course, they have been in my Bank Safe Deposit since she died. We will take them with us and you will wear them at the first official party where you will meet the Prince. The Russians, if no one else, will be aware that no ordinary English girl would possess anything so valuable and that will certainly set them thinking."

Yolisa chuckled again.

"Uncle Harold, you are wonderful! I can see your brain working all this out and you are so clever that I am sure we shall be successful."

"We have to be," her uncle said,

almost as if he was speaking to himself. "There is so much at stake. As Her Majesty knows better than anyone else, it will be a disaster impossible to put into words if the Russians achieve their objective of dominating the Aegean and the Mediterranean with their vast fleet."

Lord Langford spoke with so much feeling in his voice that Yolisa felt that it would be a mistake to ask him any more questions.

She also wanted to think over quietly what he had said to her.

And to pray that she would not make any terrible *faux pas.*

She could understand all too well the predicament that the Queen was in.

Her Majesty was unable to supply the Union Jack in the shape of a British Royal Bride for a country in such a key geographical position as Kavalla.

Yolisa had read many books about the history of Europe and she had followed with great interest the wars that had been caused by one country after another trying to seize power and expand their boundaries.

She was, in fact, well aware how dangerous Russia was at the moment.

The ambition of the last three Czars had been to gain supremacy in every direction and she had learnt that the present one, Czar Alexander III, was an exceptionally unpleasant man.

He showed none of the kindliness of his father and the moment he came to power had been unbelievably cruel to the Jews whom he hated.

Thousands had been murdered and thousands more exiled to Siberia.

She could well understand any small country being terrified of being at the mercy of such a man.

'I must try to save the Prince and his country if I can,' she told herself.

Equally the whole scenario seemed so incredible to her.

She could hardly believe it was true that she was taking part in it.

■ ■ ■ ■

She and Lord Langford had left
Warren Court soon after breakfast
and arrived in London in time for
a late luncheon.

Lord Langford's large house in
Belgrave Square was very grand
and extremely comfortable.

It had been beautifully furnished
by his wife soon after they married
and Lady Langford had with excellent taste added to it year after year.

They were always disappointed
that there had been no children of
their marriage.

Yolisa could understand why her
uncle found the big rooms so
empty and depressing now that his
wife was dead.

He therefore preferred to keep on the move about the world using his astute brain and he was asked to solve endless diplomatic and political problems that no one else could handle.

Now he was back temporarily in what had been his home since he had married.

Everything in the house, Yolisa found, went like clockwork.

Luncheon was ready for them the moment that they had arrived and the food was excellent.

As soon as they had finished, Yolisa learned that the dressmakers from Bond Street were now waiting for her upstairs.

"Do you want to see the gowns when I try them on, Uncle

Harold?" Yolisa asked.

"Of course," he replied. "I must make quite certain that they are a proper frame for your beauty and will then astound those who see you in them."

"Let's hope they will not be disappointed," Yolisa laughed as she left the room.

When she saw the gowns which were ready for her to try on upstairs, she realised at once that her uncle was determined to make her look spectacular.

Her mother would have thought that they were far too elaborate and over-decorated for a *debutante*.

She went downstairs first in an evening gown that glittered with diamanté and she twinkled like a star with every movement she made.

As she paraded herself in front of her uncle, she joked,

"At least I shall be noticed in this!"

"That is what I want," Lord Langford smiled.

He chose the gown she had on and then refused two others, choosing four altogether.

Yolisa felt that all these beautiful gowns made her look very unlike herself.

After that there were special gowns for the daytime and these were more elaborate than anything she had worn before.

There were, of course, an array of suitable hats to match them.

When Lord Langford was finally satisfied that she had enough of everything, Yolisa said nervously,

"I am sure that you are going to have an enormous bill for all this, Uncle Harold, and I think that we should ask Papa to pay some of it."

"This is to be my party," he replied, "and whatever it costs I believe it to be in a very good cause. So let's now forget that pounds, shillings and pence are involved and think only of how beautiful and impressive you are going to look."

"Then I will just say a huge 'thank you' for a very exciting present," Yolisa enthused.

She kissed her uncle's cheek.

As there was no one in the room,

he said to her,

"You are a good girl and I know I have been very wise in begging you for your help. There is no one else I could turn to at this particular moment."

"And I will be very careful not to fail you," Yolisa answered.

When the dressmakers finally left the house, it was almost time to change for dinner.

Yolisa enjoyed a bath in her bedroom and then put on one of her own gowns to go downstairs.

As she entered the drawing room, Lord Langford was thinking how lovely she was.

In fact she was so beautiful that he wondered if he was doing wrong in involving her in what might turn out to be a dangerous charade.

No one could foresee what the Russians might do next and, if it involved a murderous revolt or just a plain kidnapping, they would not hesitate.

If it suited their purpose, they were not afraid of any repercussions.

'But perhaps I am taking an unnecessary risk,' Lord Langford muttered inaudibly to himself as Yolisa walked towards him.

"I am very hungry, Uncle Harold," Yolisa said as she reached him, "but after dinner I am going straight to bed. As we are leaving tomorrow morning, I feel that I will want all my wits about me."

"You most certainly will," Lord

Langford replied. "At the same time, my dearest, I am very grateful to you for helping me."

"I only hope that is what I can do, Uncle."

He put his hand on her shoulder and said,

"From this moment we will never mention it again. When you wake up tomorrow morning, you are a Princess incognito and, when you speak to me, unless we are alone in the open air, you are talking to a man who is escorting you on Her Majesty's orders to a strange country where you will decide whether or not you will marry the reigning Prince."

Lord Langford spoke very seriously.

Yolisa listened to him with her head on one side, looking very attractive as she did so.

When he had finished, she bent forward and kissed his cheek.

"I love you, Uncle Harold," she said, "and I admire you more than I can say. I only wish that you had a son who was following you into the Diplomatic Service."

"It is something I always wanted, but then I should always be worrying about him, far more than I worry about myself."

Yolisa laughed.

"I can believe it, but you have to admit that you have had an exceedingly exciting life while many of your contemporaries have just sat at home and achieved very little."

Her eyes twinkled as she went on,

"They watched their crops in the country or risked a fortune at the gaming tables as they had nothing better to do."

Lord Langford threw back his head and chortled.

"I very much doubt if any of my friends would be complimented at what you have just said, my dearest one, although it is undoubtedly true. Now we are going into battle side by side and don't forget that after tonight you should not kiss me indiscriminately."

Yolisa laughed again.

Then, as the butler announced dinner, she slipped her arm into her uncle's and they walked together towards the dining room.

CHAPTER THREE

Lord Langford had said that he would be ready to leave the house at eleven o'clock.

Yolisa had not slept very well. She was worrying as to what she should say and what she should do on the great adventure to save Kavalla.

However, the sun was shining brightly in the sky and the birds were singing in the trees.

She put on one of the day dresses that her uncle had chosen for her and thought that it was extremely pretty.

It was the pale green of spring leaves and matched her eyes. And it also enhanced her fair hair and her white skin.

With the dress was a little jacket to match and an extremely pretty hat trimmed with flowers.

When Yolisa went downstairs, she only wished that her father could see her.

Lord Langford was waiting for her in the hall and, when she appeared, he said,

"There is no need for me to tell you that you look really lovely and our carriage is waiting."

Yolisa thanked the butler and footman for looking after her. They had carried down the stairs all the smart new trunks that her uncle had provided for her.

As they both climbed into the carriage, he handed her what looked like a large and expensive jewel case.

"You will have to carry this yourself," he said, "for the simple reason that we have not dared to bring a lady's maid with us."

"I wondered about that," Yolisa said.

"Lady Saville will help you in every way that she can and my valet, who I forgot to tell you is completely and absolutely trustworthy, will help you in any other way you may require."

He smiled before he went on,

"I would hate to tell you of how

many dangers and difficulties Dawkins has saved me from in the past. Quite frankly I would never go away without him, in the same way as I always carry a revolver."

"Now you are making me nervous!" Yolisa cried. "Are things going to be as terrifying as that?"

"No, of course not. I was only trying to make you laugh. I could see a worried expression in your eyes and I suspect that you have been awake half the night."

"If I have, do you blame me?" Yolisa enquired.

"Again, of course not. Now is the last time we can laugh and talk to each other without being afraid of being overheard."

"There has been so much to talk

about," Yolisa said, "that I have not asked you yet how we are travelling to Kavalla."

Lord Langford smiled.

"Would you be at all surprised to learn that it is in a Battleship?"

"A Battleship!" Yolisa exclaimed in astonishment.

Her uncle's eyes twinkled.

"That in itself will cause quite a sensation," he said. "Although I do realise that I am quite important, I am not usually given anything as large as a Battleship!"

Yolisa recognised at once that their arrival in such state would certainly give anyone who might be suspicious about them plenty to think about.

The Battleship was indeed duly

waiting for them on the Thames a little below Tower Bridge and Yolisa was so thrilled at the chance of seeing and actually travelling in one.

The arrangements were all definitely made in style and the Captain himself was waiting for them at the top of the gangway as they were piped onto the Battleship.

"Let me welcome you aboard *H.M.S. Victorious,* my Lord," he said to Lord Langford.

"I am very delighted to be your passenger," Lord Langford replied.

Turning to Yolisa he said,

"May I introduce Captain Graham, who commands this fine Battleship? I believe that it is the very latest new addition to the British Navy."

"That is true, my Lord," the Captain agreed, "and I and my crew are looking forward to sailing on the longest voyage we have undertaken so far."

Lord Langford smiled.

"Our other guests, my Lord," the Captain went on, "are waiting for you in the Saloon."

He then led the way and Lord Langford deliberately stood back to let Yolisa go first.

When they entered the Saloon, the two people who were waiting for them quickly rose to their feet.

Lord Langford greeted them both warmly and then introduced them to Yolisa.

Lady Saville was a small good-looking woman of nearly forty.

She made a distinct movement as if to curtsey and, then correcting herself, shook Yolisa by the hand.

Colonel Bentley, who looked exactly as an Army Officer should look, bowed lower than he would have done ordinarily.

Lord Langford then turned to the Captain,

"We are ready to go to sea, Captain, as soon as you are. I have learned from our Ambassador to Kavalla that they are eagerly looking forward to our arrival and it would be a mistake to keep them waiting for too long."

The Captain laughed.

"I will certainly try not to do that, my Lord, but no one can be certain what the sea will be like in the Bay of Biscay. But after that it should be plain sailing."

He then left the Saloon and Lord Langford chatted casually with their two fellow passengers.

Yolisa noticed, however, that they did not sit down before she was seated and they both spoke to her in a most respectful manner.

As soon as the Battleship moved into the middle of the River Thames, Lord Langford suggested to Yolisa that she might like to go below and see her cabin.

"I have told Dawkins to unpack for you," he said, "but you must tell him exactly what you will require on the voyage and what can remain in the trunks until we arrive at our destination."

Lady Saville moved towards Yolisa.

"I will help you, Your R— Lady Yolisa," she said correcting herself, "in every way I can."

"Thank you very much," Yolisa replied.

She smiled to herself, thinking that it was unlikely anyone would overhear them aboard a British Battleship at sea.

They were, however, obviously rehearsing the way they would behave when there were likely to be Russian spies watching or listening in on them.

She then went below with Lord Langford and found that she had been given the Captain's cabin, which was the largest and the most comfortable of the many cabins in the whole Battleship.

She knew that, if she had been travelling as herself, her uncle would have taken that one and she would have had a smaller cabin.

She did not make any comment, but she saw the twinkle in his eyes and knew that he was aware of what she was thinking.

As the Battleship was new, every-thing was spick and span and very up to date.

Yolisa had heard her father speak of the many new gadgets and the different type of lighting that had been introduced recently into Brit-ish Battleships.

She made a mental note to ask her uncle to show her all the innovations when he had the time.

Now she found that Dawkins was unpacking one of her trunks and, sitting down on the bed, she told him what she thought she would require on the voyage.

The trunks which contained her new evening gowns could be taken below decks and stored until they arrived.

Dawkins showed her where to put her jewel case in what he considered to be a safe place.

Yolisa had not opened it and she felt that it would be exciting to see what her uncle had brought her.

She was sure that his wife, her aunt, would have had some very valuable jewels and she was touched that he was kind enough to allow her to wear them.

He could not ask her to bring her mother's jewels without her father thinking that it was a somewhat strange request.

A *debutante's* jewels were confined to a rope of pearls and perhaps a small brooch for the front of her gown and there was no question of her wearing earrings and, of course, no rings on her fingers.

There seemed nothing more for Yolisa to do in her cabin and, having taken off her new hat and jacket, she therefore went out on deck.

It was exciting to be moving swiftly down the river and leaving London further and further behind.

'This is a real adventure,' Yolisa

told herself, 'and something I will always remember.'

That evening she enjoyed the conversation between her uncle and Colonel Bentley.

They were very careful not to speak in any personal way and yet they talked about the situation in Europe or the political difficulties at home and the way in which America as a new country was developing and expanding.

Yolisa had read about the current political situation in books and newspapers, although she had not, however, heard it actually discussed by two clever and well informed gentlemen.

They managed to bring a sense of humour into their conversation and to keep her laughing.

Lady Saville was also very intelligent and Yolisa was soon to discover that she could speak a great many languages.

And she had travelled to many parts of the world which were of little interest to most Society women.

Yolisa learned that Lady Saville had been married when she was very young and her husband had been in the Diplomatic Corps.

When he had died prematurely, she had then made herself indispensable to the Corps and because she was so good at languages she knew a great many secrets that were kept from the outside world.

"I have not yet been to Kavalla,"

she told Yolisa, "although I have in the past visited many other places in the Balkans."

"I have heard that it's a very pretty country," Yolisa said tentatively.

"And a most important one," Lady Saville replied. "I suppose you know that the Prince of Kavalla is Greek?"

"I did not realise that," Yolisa answered her.

"There was no hereditary Prince to succeed to the Throne when the last one died, so the position was offered to Prince Nikos because he had often visited Kavalla and they knew that he loved the country."

"I expect he accepted it eagerly," Yolisa remarked.

"Not exactly eagerly," Lady Saville said. "I think he knew that it would be a difficult position and, although he is a second son, he is very fond of his father's Kingdom, which is now part of Greece."

"I never thought that he might be Greek," Yolisa said, as if she was speaking to herself.

She was actually thinking about how much Greek history had always appealed to her.

She had read every book in her father's library that related stories of the many Greek Gods and Goddesses.

She also loved the writings and poetry of the many Greek Masters and her father had taught her to speak Modern Greek as he did himself.

They had actually stayed in Athens for a week on one of his journeys when he had taken her.

Yolisa had not been very old at the time, but she and her mother had been thrilled with everything they had seen and they had only been sorry that they could not stay longer.

"I would just love to visit Delphi," Yolisa now said aloud.

Lady Saville smiled.

"You must ask Prince Nikos to tell you about it. I understand that he has spent a good deal of time there."

Yolisa thought in that case they would certainly have something in common to discuss.

It might therefore not be as difficult as she had thought it would be to pretend to the Russians that she was considering him as her future husband.

The Bay of Biscay turned out to be not as rough as the Captain had feared.

Although it was unwise to walk about on the deck, Yolisa enjoyed seeing the huge waves breaking over the bow of the Battleship.

She was impressed by the way that *The Victorious* stood up to them.

On the fourth day out she was sitting alone in the Saloon reading the newspapers that had come aboard at Gibraltar.

One of the Stewards came in carrying a tray and she took no notice of him until he came over to her side to ask,

"Is there anything I can get you, my Lady? A glass of lemonade or perhaps something stronger?"

"Nothing, thank you," Yolisa replied. "And it will soon be time for luncheon."

"His Lordship ordered luncheon for one o'clock," the Steward said, "and it will, of course, be precisely on time."

Yolisa thought that he spoke very good English for a Steward.

Then, as he walked away, she had the feeling that there was something strange about him.

She could not explain it, because

he looked quite ordinary. In fact he was rather a plain man and not very tall.

When it was time for luncheon, the others joined her in the Saloon.

She was at the same time very aware of the Steward bringing in the food and serving it with the help of the other Stewards.

She waited until she was alone with her uncle on deck.

Then, as they bent over the railings, she moved just a little closer to him.

"I may be wrong, Uncle Harold," she said, "but I think there is something strange about the Steward they call 'William'."

"The Steward?" Lord Langford questioned her in surprise. "Have you had any contact with him?"

"He asked me before luncheon-time if there was anything I wanted," Yolisa answered. "I noticed he spoke remarkably good English, unlike the others, and I then had a definite feeling about him."

She gave a little laugh before she added,

"I was using what Papa calls my *Third Eye* and, of course, I may be wrong."

"You are quite right to tell me," Lord Langford said. "I will make some enquiries or rather I will tell the Colonel to do so."

When he left her, Yolisa thought that she was being rather foolish.

How was it possible that there

could be a Russian spy on board a British Battleship?

But her uncle had told her to trust her intuition.

She was certainly aware of William in a way that she did not feel for any of the other Stewards.

Late that evening they both went out on deck after dinner.

As Yolisa gazed at the lights on the distant coast, Lord Langford said in a low voice,

"You were absolutely correct about William. The Captain took him on just before this voyage because the Steward who should have sailed with us was taken ill."

He looked around him before he added,

"That was what Captain was told.

But now Bentley and I suspect that his illness might have been caused by something he was given or by what he was paid."

"What do you mean, Uncle?" Yolisa asked.

"The man sent a message to the ship saying that he was ill twenty-four hours before we were due to sail. It would obviously be very difficult for the Captain to find a replacement. One of the other Stewards, however, said that he had a friend he had known for some time and who had been a Steward on several Trans-Atlantic Steamers."

"And that was William!" Yolisa exclaimed.

"Exactly. So William appeared

and we now suspect that we have a Russian spy aboard."

"I can hardly believe it!" Yolisa cried.

"I have told you they are everywhere and they are extremely proficient. Their spies can speak perfectly in a great number of languages and they creep into everything however hard one tries to keep them out."

"What will you do about William," Yolisa asked.

"Nothing will be done while we are at sea," Lord Langford said. "But when *The Victorious* reaches Kavalla, William will be told by the Captain that his services are no longer required."

"Just that?" Yolisa queried.

"Just that. He has done nothing wrong, in fact he has carried out his duties admirably. But a report of who we are and what we have said will be received by The Third Section in St. Petersburg, who will undoubtedly take a great interest in you."

Yolisa shivered.

She well knew that The Third Section of the Secret Police, which had been introduced in 1825, was feared not only by other countries but by everyone in Russia.

Czar Alexander III had increased its activities and its power from the moment that he came to the Throne in Russia.

It was spreading its tentacles like a giant octopus all over Europe.

The mere fact that a Russian was on board created an atmosphere that Yolisa was extremely conscious of.

For the first few days of the voyage she had thought that her uncle gradually became less intense. And Lady Saville and Colonel Bentley were really at their ease and not just pretending.

But after they had learned that William was suspect they became a great deal more wary and especially more careful of what they said at meal times.

Yolisa saw that they were all on their guard in the Saloon and elsewhere on board ship just in case a listening device had been installed without anyone's knowledge.

It gave her a creepy feeling.

When she went to her own cabin, she wondered if that too had been tampered with.

'Perhaps I am exaggerating the whole threat!' she tried to think.

At the same time she knew if she was honest that she only felt free when she was in the open air.

As her uncle had insisted, it was the only safe place where she could speak without being afraid.

Now, as they were in a hurry to reach Kavalla, the Battleship moved ahead at full speed.

They did not call at Malta or at any other Port on their route

Yet Yolisa hoped that there would be a chance of going ashore at Athens, but they only stopped to pick up fuel, newspapers and letters. No one except the Captain was allowed ashore.

"I hoped that I would be able to see Athens again," Yolisa said to her uncle rather wistfully.

"Perhaps you will do that on our return home," he answered.

"Oh, do let's try to go ashore then," Yolisa begged him.

"Perhaps it will be a prize for being a good girl," her uncle answered. "Because that is important I will make it an added inducement!"

"Added?" Yolisa quizzed, "to what?"

Her uncle smiled.

"That is a secret. But I do promise you that we are not stingy with our rewards for people who help us in the Diplomatic game."

He would not say anything more, but Yolisa knew that he was pleased by the way she had acted so far.

Because they were now suspicious of William, they put on a special performance for his benefit.

From then on every evening either Lady Saville or Colonel Bentley hesitated when they addressed Yolisa.

When she said "goodnight" or left the Saloon, they hurried to their feet and once Lady Saville stumbled as if she was about to curtsey when she hoped that she would sleep well.

It was such an uncomfortable feeling to know that William, if he

was on duty, was watching everything that was happening.

'At least,' Yolisa told herself, 'it
will make the Russians aware of my
importance even before I arrive in
Kavalla.'

They sailed up the Aegean Sea,
passing the many small Greek Is-
lands, all of which had fascinating
histories and customs.

Yolisa wished so much that her
father was with her to tell her more
about them.

She knew that her uncle, even
with his knowledge of the world,
would not be able to answer her
questions as interestingly or as
clearly as her father could.

'I am being greedy,' she told herself. 'I have so much, but am still

asking for more.'

What she really wanted to know was all about Kavalla and its Prince.

When she tried to question Lord Langford, he said evasively,

"I want you to give me your first impressions when you have arrived and for them to be exactly what you feel yourself, uninfluenced by anything you have been told by me or anyone else."

"I know what you are saying to me," Yolisa replied. "But it is all so exciting that I am frightened of missing something of interest simply through ignorance or lack of prior briefing."

"I am very certain you will not," Lord Langford replied, "and, with regard to the history of Kavalla, there will be a great number of people in the Palace only too willing to bore you with the whole rigmarole of its history, if that is what you want to hear."

"I realise that you are deliberately trying to prevent me from knowing too much until I actually arrive," Yolisa laughed.

"Now that you are using your *Third Eye,*" Lord Langford replied, "and that is what I wish you to do, I want you to come fresh to the whole problem which lies ahead of us and perhaps that will help you to be cleverer than we have been."

"I think you are making it rather more difficult than it need be," Yolisa complained. "After all, we know who our enemies are and any Russian, rich or poor, is clearly under suspicion."

"It's not as easy as it sounds, Yolisa. For instance, while William is undoubtedly working for the Russians, he is not actually a Russian."

Yolisa looked surprised.

"I thought that he must be."

"That is where you are wrong. He is an extremely clever Pole, who has found it to his advantage to work for the Russians. I would not be surprised if he is not in some way a part of The Third Section."

"And if he is," Yolisa said, "his Masters, by getting him on board this ship, are telling us how important they think you are."

"There I do agree with you," he replied, "and I am only thankful that we have acted our parts from the first minute we came aboard the ship. That has undoubtedly given William a great deal to report to those who arranged for him to be a Steward."

It was an intriguing thought, but at the same time frightening.

Yolisa now felt that she would be glad when their voyage came to an end.

It was a warm sunny day when they steamed into Port.

Yolisa had her first look at the Capital City of the country.

She had learned already from her uncle that it was where the Royal

Palace was situated.

Because the Port was of great strategic value, it was one that the Russians especially wished to get their greedy hands on.

Ostensibly it was Lord Langford who was the most important visitor.

He was greeted by the British Ambassador and the Secretary of State of Kavalla for Foreign Affairs and there were also a good number of other dignitaries waiting for them.

After a welcome consisting of a long speech from one of the dignitaries, open carriages each drawn by four white horses escorted by a troop of mounted Cavalrymen took them to the Palace.

Yolisa wondered if the ordinary Statesmen and the *aides-de-camp* in attendance at the Royal Palace thought it strange that so much fuss was being made for a man who was just a well-known British Diplomat.

It was impossible, however, to ask any questions.

Yolisa and Lord Langford drove in one carriage with the British Ambassador and the Kavallean Secretary of State for Foreign Affairs and so their conversation was formal and stilted.

There were questions about the smoothness of the sea, the health of Her Majesty Queen Victoria and the preparations for her Golden Jubilee which was taking place that year.

Yolisa thought with amusement that the same kind of conversation must be repeated over and over again when representatives of other countries arrived.

She noticed the children along the route who waved excitedly as they passed by, but the men and women just stood and stared at them.

The people seemed very strong and healthy and the children, she thought, were very attractive.

There was no sign of poverty, if it existed at all, and she had a glimpse of the shops and they appeared to be filled with goods to sell.

The people passing in and out of them or looking in the windows were well dressed.

The streets were lined with trees and there seemed to be a profusion of flowers everywhere

In fact it was an exceedingly pretty City.

To make herself pleasant Yolisa bent forward to the Secretary of State and said to him,

"Your people here look prosperous and happy. I hope that is true throughout the whole country."

"It is at this moment," he replied, "and long may it remain so."

There was unmistakably a note of doubt in the way he spoke.

They drove on and at last Yolisa had her first sight of the Palace.

It was situated high up above the City and painted white and half encircled by exotic trees which were all in bloom.

It was so lovely that she gave an exclamation of astonishment and the Secretary of State told her proudly,

"Everyone is thrilled when they see our Palace. In fact a number of Royal visitors have been jealous because it is finer than the Palaces they have themselves."

"I think it is so beautiful," Yolisa enthused.

She became even more impressed when they drove nearer.

In the gardens which sloped down from the Palace to the road there were four huge fountains throwing their water up to the sky.

There was a long flight of steps from the Palace down to the road beneath it.

But they did not have to climb them. Instead they drove on up a road that led up to one side of the Palace.

At a most impressive entrance there were sentries on duty and a red carpet over the steps.

Inside the front door there were a great number of extravagantly liveried servants in attendance.

The Lord Chamberlain himself was waiting to greet them.

"Welcome, my Lord," he boomed. "It is delightful to have you with us again in Kavalla."

"My niece and I are most gratified," Lord Langford replied, "to be the guests of His Royal Highness."

"Prince Nikos is most impressed by Great Britain," the Lord Chamberlain answered, "and is a great admirer of Her Majesty Queen Victoria. He has a special present for you to take back with you on your return home when I understand that she is celebrating the fiftieth year of her reign."

"That is true," Lord Langford agreed, "and I am sure that Her Majesty will be delighted to receive a present from Kavalla."

The Lord Chamberlain led them into a Great Hall where there were more Officials to greet them.

Yolisa noticed that most of them were very good-looking men and taller than she had expected.

Then they were ushered through

a number of large and well-furnished rooms until they came to what Yolisa guessed were the private apartments of the Prince.

By this time their extensive entourage had shrunk considerably and they were now being led only by the Lord Chamberlain and the British Ambassador.

Meanwhile Lady Saville and Colonel Bentley were being looked after by other Officials.

There were two footmen standing outside a door that was surmounted by the Royal Emblem of Kavalla.

When the procession appeared, they flung open the door and another servant inside bowed.

The Lord Chamberlain then went

ahead and they followed him.

As Yolisa had expected, it was quite obviously the Prince's private study. It was furnished with comfortable chairs and sofas beside a great display of flowers.

The Prince was at the far end of the room sitting in a chair reading a newspaper and, as the Lord Chamberlain entered, he rose to his feet.

As he walked towards them, Yolisa was aware that her uncle had been absolutely right in describing him as "Prince Charming".

He was tall, dark and exceedingly handsome.

In fact one of the best-looking men she had ever seen.

As she moved towards him, she

was aware that he was not only smiling but his eyes were twinkling.

She knew that he was thinking, as she did, that this whole charade was quite unreal and part of a Fairytale.

"May I present, Your Royal Highness," the Lord Chamberlain was saying, "Lady Yolisa Ford, who has just arrived from England."

"I am very delighted to see you, Lady Yolisa," the Prince declared and put out his hand.

As she took it, Yolisa swept into a deep curtsey.

At the same time because she was feeling nervous her fingers trembled in his.

Then, as she looked up into his eyes, she knew that he was different, very different from any man she had ever come across before.

"May I also present," the Lord Chamberlain was saying, "Lord Langford, whom Your Royal Highness has met before."

"Of course I have," the Prince replied, "and it is so delightful, my Lord, to welcome you back to Kavalla."

"I am not only charmed to be in your beautiful country again," Lord Langford said, "but to bring with me my niece, who has already been admiring the beauty of the City and its inhabitants."

"Which I do hope includes me," the Prince smiled. "Come and sit down, my Lord, and give me the latest news from England."

He walked towards the chair where he had been sitting before they had arrived, while the Lord Chamberlain faded into the background.

They then sat down and the Prince started to ask questions about the Queen's Jubilee and the celebrations being arranged in London.

As Lord Langford answered him, Yolisa was aware that he was gazing at her.

She was not certain whether it was because he was curious or because he wanted anyone who was watching him to be aware of his interest in her.

She had previously asked her uncle if the Prince knew what they were doing.

"Of course he does," he asserted. "But no one else in the Palace has the slightest idea that there is any ulterior motive in your visit to Kavalla."

"So everyone but the Prince will assume that you have brought me with you, as your niece, as just a plain ordinary visitor."

"Exactly. It would be impossible to tell any one of his people without telling them all," Lord Langford said. "And, if only one of the Statesmen told his wife because it was such a good story, she would be unable to keep it to herself."

"I think that is unkind. But I expect it's the truth," Yolisa laughed.

"Women are always quite a risk when it comes to secrets," Lord Langford had said somewhat provocatively. "Therefore the Prime Minister and I entrusted a man from the Foreign Office to go ahead of us and inform the Prince secretly what we are planning."

He smiled before he continued,

"Of course, he naturally will be disappointed that there is no possibility of his having an English wife until another year at least has passed."

Later, when Yolisa was talking to her uncle, she said,

"I suppose it is impossible to conceive of any other way that the Prince can save his country except by being married to an Englishwoman of Royal blood."

"If there is another way, then you think of it," Lord Langford replied. "I suppose every Statesman in the world has racked his brains to think of how to prevent Russia expanding as she is doing at the moment. No one wants to go to war, yet there seems no other way of stopping her from grabbing every small country on her borders."

Watching the Prince now when he was talking to her uncle, Yolisa wondered what he really felt.

He would marry a woman he had never seen and with whom he might have no interests in common.

She felt certain that there must have been plenty of women in his life already. He was far too hand-some not to have been pursued, even if he himself was not the pursuer, by almost every woman he met.

She knew from what she had read that the Greeks had a special charm which most women found irresist-ible.

'What country could be more romantic?' she asked herself.

Unexpectedly the Prince turned to speak to her.

"Your uncle tells me, Lady Yolisa," he said, "that you have visited Athens. Tell me what you thought of the land I belong to."

"It is not only beautiful," Yolisa replied, "but it is romantic, excit-ing and totally compelling."

She spoke the last three words in Greek and the Prince remarked,

"So you speak my language?"

He asked the question in Greek and then Yolisa answered him in the same language,

"I learned it because it's so beautiful."

"Just as you are," the Prince replied.

They smiled at each other.

Yolisa was then aware that the Lord Chamberlain and her uncle had not understood what they had said to each other.

Lord Langford spoke a little Greek, but he found it difficult to follow a conversation.

Now, as if he realised this, the Prince said to him,

"I find it very surprising, Lord Langford, that your niece should be so accomplished as to speak my native language, which is a difficult one. I think she will find it easy to make herself understood in Kavalla. Our language here is a combination of several European languages which are considered fairly easy."

"I agree with you," Lord Langford said. "I have had very little difficulty in making myself understood in Kavalla. But with your Ancient Greek and Modern Greek I am often at sea."

The Prince laughed.

"That is quite an admission, my Lord, that I did not expect to hear from you!"

"I assure Your Royal Highness that I am always strictly truthful," Lord Langford commented.

His eyes met the Prince's as he spoke.

They were both thinking about the charade they were acting at the moment and wondered if it would be successful.

The Prince rose to his feet.

"I am hoping, my Lord," he said, "that you and Lady Yolisa will join me at dinner tonight and tomorrow I would like you both to be present at a Military Parade. It will take place in the City and we are paying a special tribute to your English Queen."

"That is most gracious of Your Royal Highness," Lord Langford said, "and I am that sure Her Majesty will be very touched by your thought for her."

"I know you will carry an account of what happens back to England with you," the Prince said, "and I should be surprised if many countries do not follow our lead in sending her not only our good wishes but also a present to add to what must be, by this time, a very large collection at Windsor Castle."

Lord Langford chuckled.

"That is true, Your Royal Highness, but then there is always room for more."

"So until this evening, my Lord," the Prince said.

He shook Lord Langford's hand as he bowed and then turned to

Yolisa.

Once again she curtseyed.

As his fingers closed over hers, she had a strange feeling within her breast that she had never known before.

She could not explain it to herself, but it was there.

Then, as they walked away towards the door, she was very aware, although she had her back to him, that the Prince's eyes were following her.

It gave her a strange and unusual feeling.

She felt as if she had met him, not for the first time, but he had somehow been there in her life all down the centuries.

CHAPTER FOUR

When they went up the stairs to change for dinner, Yolisa was surprised to find that they were in the Royal Apartments.

She realised that it was so because there were two sentries on duty outside the door and she had not seen them in the other parts of the Palace.

She was aware, without his saying so, that her uncle was amused.

The Royal Apartments were more spectacular than the rest of the

Palace and they were situated at one end of the huge building.

As they were taken upstairs by an *aide-de-camp,* Yolisa could see that the pictures were even finer and more spectacular than any she had seen elsewhere in the Palace.

It seemed to be particularly quiet and, almost as if the *aide-de-camp* knew that she was surprised, he told her,

"Only His Royal Highness's special friends stay in this part of the Palace and you and your niece, my Lord, are the only guests we have had here so far this year."

"Then, of course, we are indeed very honoured," Lord Langford replied diplomatically.

The top of the stairs led them into

a wide corridor. It was furnished with the most exquisite chests inlaid with mother-of-pearl.

The *aide-de-camp* opened a door halfway down it.

"This room is for you, my Lady," he said to Yolisa, "and your boudoir is next door."

Before Yolisa could enter her room, the *aide-de-camp* crossed the corridor to a door opposite.

"And this, my Lord," he added, "is your room. I think you will enjoy knowing that it is named after one of the great heroes of Kavalla."

"Then I hope I will emulate him," Lord Langford grinned.

Yolisa had a brief glimpse of Dawkins unpacking her uncle's trunks and then turned towards her own room.

As she did so, the *aide-de-camp* suggested,

"If there is anything that you require, my Lady, you have a bell in your room which rings for the housekeeper, and, of course, if for any reason you are nervous, there are always sentries on duty at the entrance to the apartments."

"That is very comforting," Yolisa replied.

And she could see that he was looking at her with admiration in his eyes.

She smiled at him before she added,

"Thank you very much for looking after us."

"It's a great pleasure," the *aide-de-camp* said, "and I can promise that the whole City will be waiting to see you tomorrow."

Yolisa smiled at him again and then went into her own room.

There were two maidservants busily unpacking her gowns and hanging them carefully in a beautifully carved wardrobe.

They rose as she entered and bobbed her a curtsey.

She greeted them a little hesitatingly in their own language, which she had been studying on the journey.

It was, she found, a mixture of Greek, Hungarian and, she thought, a bit of German.

It was therefore not very difficult

for her to say at least a few words that the maids understood.

They were delighted and one of them clapped her hands and exclaimed,

"My Lady speak like us. That is good, very good!"

"But it's rather more difficult for me to understand you," Yolisa said, "but I am sure I shall soon get better."

Actually she found that she could understand quite a lot of what they said as they continued unpacking.

She had learned a good deal from Lady Saville and she would be able to rely on her for help if she could not make herself understood.

Now it was very obvious that only her uncle and she were to be privileged enough to be staying in the Royal Apartments.

Lady Saville therefore might well be sleeping some distance away.

'I am sure that I can manage,' Yolisa told herself.

As there was now plenty of time before dinner, she then explored her boudoir. It had a communicating door opening out of her bedroom.

It was a large and very attractive room, containing some outstandingly beautiful furniture and here too there were pictures that she knew her father would have loved to have seen.

There was also a bookcase at one end of the room.

Yolisa told herself severely that

she must not look at the books
now. If she did, she would undoubtedly be late for dinner.

When she went back into her
bedroom, the maids had finished
unpacking.

They were now bringing in the
bath that they were setting down in
front of the fireplace.

They then helped Yolisa undress
and waited on her while she bathed,
while she thought that whoever ran
the Palace must be very efficient.

There was a scented oil to pour
into the water and the bath was
exactly the right temperature and
the towels to dry herself with were
soft and absorbent.

Yolisa also noticed that there were
small luxuries which she expected

to find in English country houses but not in foreign ones.

There were biscuits beside the bed in case she was hungry at night and fresh water was available in a crystal jug.

Besides the candles in a gold candelabra, there was a small lantern in case she wanted to move about in the night.

The maids helped her put on her underclothes. Then they opened the wardrobe where they had hung her gowns and waited for her to choose the one she would wear.

For a moment Yolisa hesitated.

She had no idea what she would have to do in the next few days and she wondered which of the dresses her uncle had chosen for her was the most spectacular.

Then she remembered her father saying once, *'first impressions are always important.'*

So she pointed to the gown that had diamanté glittering all over it.

'If nothing else,' she thought, 'everybody will have to notice me.'

One of the maids was obviously particularly skilful in hairdressing and arranged Yolisa's beautifully.

When she had put on her gown, she remembered the jewellery and, because she was not used to wearing jewels, she had not given them a thought.

She had not even opened the case while she was aboard *H.M.S. Victorious.*

She found now that the jewel case

had been brought upstairs and set down beside her dressing table.

The key was in her handbag and, as she opened it, she was curious as to what she would find.

At the first glance she was stunned by an enormous diamond necklace. It was far bigger than the one that her mother had owned or any necklace she had seen on any of her parents' friends.

She then remembered that her uncle had told her that he had spent some time with the Nizam of Hyderabad while he had been in India.

The richest man in India, he had a diamond mine that was all his own and she was sure that was where the diamonds must have come from and they were certainly amazing.

Yet she thought that it would be too much to wear tonight, especially as her gown was already glittering with diamanté.

She found another necklace, also of diamonds, but not so large and she thought that it too must have come from India.

She then put it on and discovered that there were earrings to go with it as well as a bracelet.

When she then looked at herself in the mirror, she wanted to laugh.

If she needed to be spectacular, she had certainly succeeded!

She was quite sure, however, that her mother would have thought that she was very overdressed.

'If this does not impress the Prince,' she said to herself, 'it will certainly make the Russians sit up and take notice of me.'

Once again she felt a little shiver go through her.

It was frightening to think that everything she did and perhaps everything she said was being reported.

If not to The Third Section, then certainly to the Russian who was in control of this particular operation.

'They will be very certain after tonight,' Yolisa told herself, 'that if I have jewels like these I must be Royal.'

Because she felt defiant she then added a smaller bracelet, which was also of diamonds, to her other wrist.

The two maids were regarding her with awe and they paid her compliments in their own language.

Yolisa was wondering whether she should go to her uncle's room when there came a knock on the door.

"May I come in?" Lord Langford asked.

"Yes, of course, Uncle Harold."

He then entered the room looking very smart in his evening clothes on which were pinned a number of his decorations. There was also a large cross round his neck suspended on a red ribbon.

She had never before seen him dressed so formally.

And, before she could tell him

what she thought, he exclaimed,

"You look exactly as I want you to!"

The maids had tactfully left the room so that they were alone and Yolisa said in a very low voice,

"Thank you for these wonderful diamonds."

"I just knew they would become you," he replied.

There was, however, she thought, a pain in his eyes.

She was certain that he was remembering who had worn them last and wishing that it was his wife who stood there rather than his niece.

Yolisa slipped her hand in his.

"I am so glad you approve of me, Uncle Harold," she said, "and thank you very very much."

"Then let's go downstairs," he said. "It will amuse me to see how overcome they will be by your appearance."

"I am very impressed that we have been given these particular rooms," Yolisa whispered.

"So am I," her uncle replied. "At the same time remember it is exactly what you are entitled to."

"Of course," Yolisa agreed with a smile.

They walked to the top of the stairs and then her uncle gave her his arm and then they went down slowly and with dignity.

There was an *aide-de-camp* waiting at the foot of the stairs.

He was to lead them to where the

Reception for the Banquet was to take place.

It was in the formal part of the Palace and there were more guests than Yolisa had expected and they were all chattering to each other somewhat noisily and drinking champagne.

When she and Lord Langford came into the room, there was a sudden hush.

Then the Prince came forward to greet them.

As he did so, Yolisa was aware of the astonishment in the eyes of the ladies and the admiration in those of the gentlemen.

Again she took the Prince's hand and curtseyed to him.

If she thought that her uncle

looked magnificent, the Prince was more so.

He was wearing a blue ribbon over one shoulder and all the stars glittering with diamonds on his white coat were dazzling.

He seemed even taller and more overpowering than he had when they first met.

Yolisa thought that it would be impossible to find any man who was more handsome and he could truly be described as looking like a Greek God.

The Prince then presented to her a number of the Statesmen who had not met them when they had arrived at the Palace.

The more Yolisa spoke in the language of Kavalla and the more she listened to it, the easier she found it. In fact it was quite unnecessary for the Statesmen to talk to her in broken English.

When they went into dinner, it was the Prince who gave her his arm and she found that she was sitting on his right.

She knew immediately that this would cause a huge amount of comment amongst the other guests.

She realised that the Prince himself was finding the situation amusing.

'If they are not all talking about me tomorrow,' Yolisa said to herself, 'it will certainly not be my fault!'

The dining room was as impressive as the rest of the Palace. The long table with golden candlesticks and a magnificent display of goblets inset with many jewels was something that Yolisa had never seen before.

In between the ornaments there were rare orchids skilfully arranged and bowls of *Sèvres* porcelain filled with fruit.

"Your Palace is just like a Fairy Palace, Your Royal Highness," she remarked to the Prince soon after they were seated.

"I just hoped that that was what you would think," he replied.

"So, if the rest of your country is equally beautiful," Yolisa said, "then you are obviously the most fortunate man in the whole world."

Without thinking, as he was looking so Greek, she spoke to him in

Modern Greek.

He replied to her in the same language.

"I will show you some of my country tomorrow and I am quite certain that you like riding."

"I would rather ride than do anything else," Yolisa replied. "I am sure that your horses are as magnificent as your Palace."

"I hope you will think so," the Prince said. "As it happens, they come from Hungary."

Yolisa laughed.

"Then you certainly have the best. My father, who is a most experienced horseman, has always told me that the finest horses he has ever ridden have been Hungarian."

"I thought, if it suited you," the Prince replied, still speaking in Greek, "we could ride off early in the morning before all the arduous duties of the day start."

"In England I usually ride before breakfast," Yolisa volunteered.

"That is what I thought you would do," the Prince said. "A Hungarian horse will be waiting for you at half-past seven, if that is not too early."

"This is an excitement I was not expecting, Sire," Yolisa answered. "And I promise I will not be late."

"I feel that you always keep your promises," the Prince said, "and it is something I try hard to do myself."

Yolisa was thinking to herself that

everything was so different from what she had expected. She had somehow thought that the Prince's Palace would be quite small and its furnishings not particularly fine.

She had reckoned that the Prince would be a good-looking man, but not so overwhelmingly handsome.

Now she was to ride Hungarian horses with him!

That was very different from travelling in pomp in an open carriage!

She felt her heart leap with anticipation.

"I know just what you are thinking," the Prince said unexpectedly. "Although I consider it an insult, I am glad to have surprised you."

Yolisa turned to look at him in astonishment.

"You are reading my thoughts!" she exclaimed.

"I confess that I am," the Prince replied, "and I find them very intriguing."

"It is something that Your Royal Highness should not do," Yolisa protested. "But I suppose it is because you are Greek that you can do so."

"It is something I only do on special occasions," the Prince grinned. "And then what can be more special than meeting you?"

Yolisa felt that he was being very complimentary and she responded,

"I think actually, Sire, that is exactly what I should be saying to Your Royal Highness and what you would indeed expect."

The Prince laughed.

"Now you are pretending to be modest, which is quite unnecessary. Do tell me what you felt when you first touched my hand."

Yolisa's eyes widened.

"Why do you ask?" she questioned.

"Because I knew at once that you felt what you did not expect and I felt the same."

Yolisa was so surprised that she stared at him and then quickly looked away.

Ever since she had entered the room she had been conscious of the Prince in a way that she did not wish to explain to herself.

When he had come forward to greet her, she felt for a second that he was enveloped with a dazzling light.

And it seemed to stream continuously from him.

Then she told herself that she must be charming and concentrate herself on creating a good impression which was expected.

At the same time showing a Royal reserve towards those she was introduced to.

She tried not to think about the Prince.

Yet now, when they were seated side by side, she found herself vividly conscious of his closeness to her in a way that she could not understand.

She could feel his vibrations pouring out from him and meeting hers.

In a strange way they were united as one.

They were talking together, yet the words seemed unimportant.

He was there beside her and she was with him.

That made what they were saying seem to be of little consequence compared with their life force.

All this flashed instantaneously through her mind.

Then, as she looked up and her eyes met his, he said very quietly,

"It is exactly what I am feeling too, so now you understand."

She was frightened by what he said.

And by the strange effect he had on her heart — or was it her mind — she was not certain which.

Yolisa deliberately turned away.

She began to talk animatedly to the Prime Minister who was on her other side.

She asked him about the country and then about the Army.

"Have you a large Army in Kavalla?" she enquired.

"It's not as big as His Royal Highness would like," the Prime Minister replied. "In fact we are recruiting more and more men, but we are only a small country and large Armies are a great expense."

"But they are protective," Yolisa said positively.

"I agree," the Prime Minister answered. "That is why His Royal Highness is anxious that we should possess not only the newest and most up to date weapons available as well as the vital protection of Great Britain."

Yolisa smiled.

"That is something I do hope you will soon have," she replied.

She did not say anything more because she was not certain if the Prime Minister knew about the game that they were playing.

He might easily have been deceived into believing that she was, in fact, a Princess in disguise.

Whatever it might be, Yolisa realised that she had already aroused a great deal of curiosity amongst the other guests.

She thought that, if this was what her uncle desired, he had certainly been successful.

Like the French, but unlike the English, the ladies and gentlemen left the dinner table together.

They moved back to the large Reception room in which they had met before dinner and now there was a small orchestra playing, although no one was expected to sit down and listen to it.

The ladies were all very anxious to talk to Yolisa and she then moved amongst them trying to make herself agreeable.

Equally she appeared to be somewhat aloof if asked questions that were too intimate and it was quite a difficult part for her to play.

She was relieved when it grew late enough for the Prince to withdraw.

He said 'goodnight' to Lord Langford and then he turned towards Yolisa.

He put out his hand and she sank down in a deep curtsey.

His fingers tightened on hers.

Once again she felt that strange feeling, which had swept through her at their first meeting.

This time it was more intense and it was something not only unprecedented but also exceedingly exciting.

Then, as Yolisa looked up to the Prince's eyes, she was aware that he was feeling exactly the same.

She could not explain how she knew this.

The two of them were united for the moment by a spiritual force which was quite inexplicable.

Almost as if he forced himself to speak, the Prince said softly so that only she could hear,

"Tomorrow morning."

Then he was gone and Yolisa felt as if all the lights had been extinguished.

Almost as if she was in a haze, she went upstairs with her uncle.

Everything was very quiet in their apartments once they had passed through the door guarded by the uniformed sentries.

Her uncle walked into her bedroom behind her.

"I need not tell you," he said, "how brilliantly you behaved tonight and just how impressed everyone was with you."

"I did my best, Uncle," Yolisa

murmured.

"Go to bed and don't worry about anything," Lord Langford said. "Tomorrow will certainly be an exhausting Parade. You will walk on a tightrope and do it better than anyone has ever done before."

"That is exactly what I want you to say," Yolisa sighed.

"Goodnight," her uncle called walking towards the door.

He did not kiss her and Yolisa thought that he was keeping up the pretence that she was a Princess disguised to be his niece.

However clever the Russians might be, she did not believe that they could manage to penetrate so far into the Palace.

Nor to have any secret means of

listening to what she said in this bedroom.

However, as her uncle closed the door and left her alone, she felt that he was wise just in case the Russians had found some secret means of listening or looking in on them without anyone being aware of it.

Yolisa then rang for the maid as she had been told to do.

The maid who had looked after her before came hurrying in.

"Everyone's talkin' about you, gracious lady," she said as she undid Yolisa's gown.

"What did they say?" Yolisa enquired.

"They say you're either an angel from Heaven or a Goddess from the country that His Royal Highness comes from."

Yolisa laughed.

"A Goddess!" she exclaimed. "That is indeed a compliment! Then I wonder which Goddess I would like to be."

When she climbed into her bed, however, she was thinking of the Prince and reflecting on which of the Gods he most resembled.

She felt certain that the women in his life, and of course there must have been a number of them, would have told him that he looked like a Greek God.

It would be difficult to decide which one would be most appropriate for him.

She found herself again thinking of the strange way that the Prince had talked to her.

How could he possibly have felt as she had when they first met?

How could he read her thoughts and so understand what she was trying to say?

It was all very intriguing.

Yet some sensible part of her mind told her that she must not become too involved with him.

To him she was just a ship that was passing in the night.

When she returned home to England, she would have carried through the complicated task that her uncle had planned for her.

Then the Prince would never think about her again.

Yet she undoubtedly would now find it hard to be attracted to the ordinary Englishmen her father wanted her to meet in London.

They would talk about their horses, their country houses and the problems on their estates.

Inevitably she would then compare them with the Prince talking about Gods and Goddesses.

With all the strange vibrations emanating from him that she could not explain and their reading of each other's thoughts.

'I am sensible enough,' Yolisa said to herself, 'to know that this is dangerous. If I did fall in love with the Prince, which is something I would never have imagined doing in a thousand years, I shall then go back to England a "Miss Nobody", who has left her heart behind in a small but politically important country.'

She closed her eyes.

It would be a great mistake to go riding with the Prince tomorrow morning!

If she was prudent, she would say that she was too tired.

She could then just meet him at the first public engagement they had together.

But even as she thought about it, she knew that was something she could not do.

It would be a great mistake to insult the Prince the moment she had arrived in his country.

She had expected danger, if there was any, to come from the Russians.

Or perhaps the danger of being publicly exposed as an imposter.

Now she was aware of another danger.

A danger that came from within herself!

She was trying to disregard it, but she was forced to admit that it was a turn of events she had never expected.

It could easily be exceedingly dangerous in a very different way.

And even as she argued with herself, she knew that it was quite hopeless.

Just how could any girl, living as quietly as she had always done in the depths of the country, refuse what she was now apparently being offered?

A Prince of a Fairytale country!

A magnificent Hungarian horse to ride!

Something completely irresistibly new, unexpected and very intriguing now happening between herself and the most handsome man she had ever seen.

"It cannot be true," Yolisa murmured aloud. "I am dreaming and tomorrow morning I shall wake up."

Eventually she fell into a deep sleep.

When she awoke, the sun was shining through the sides of the curtains.

A few minutes later the maid she had told to call her came into the room.

Yolisa had allowed herself half an hour to dress in and she was ready at a quarter past seven.

Among the clothes she had brought from home was a riding habit that was almost new.

She had grown out of the one that she had worn for several years and her father had then insisted that she went to the best tailor in the County.

He told her to order a habit that was well-cut and fitted without a wrinkle.

He was very particular about what he wore himself when he was riding and he disliked women who looked untidy or who had badly fitting habits.

When Yolisa was dressed, she thought that anyone who might have criticised her appearance last night would have to admit that she was absolutely correct this morning.

She was not surprised when there came a knock on the door.

There was an *aide-de-camp* outside to take her on His Royal Highness's instructions to where the horses were waiting.

Yolisa was aware that neither her uncle nor anyone else knew what was happening this morning.

She was taken down a side passage to a door that opened out at the back of the Palace.

She expected the horses to be waiting there, but to her surprise the *aide-de-camp* went on until they reached the stables.

The Prince was there talking with a man who was obviously a Head Groom and there were six horses being paraded in front of him.

At the sight of him Yolisa felt as if her heart turned a somersault.

And, as he looked towards her, she was almost sure that he felt the same.

"Good morning, Lady Yolisa," he greeted her as she curtseyed. "You are very punctual. I wanted to see which of these horses you would prefer."

"Am I to have a choice, Sire?" Yolisa asked.

"But of course," he replied. "Let me tell you that they are all Hungarian and I will not say which of the six I myself like best."

"That is very generous," Yolisa replied, "but I shall feel embarrassed, Sire, if I choose the one you really want to ride yourself."

"I will risk your being clever enough to choose it," the Prince smiled. "But you must concentrate on the horse and not on my mind."

Remembering the conversation that they had had at dinner, Yolisa laughed.

"I will try not to cheat," she promised.

She carefully examined all the six horses.

They were all exceptional and just what she thought Hungarian horses should be like.

She had always longed to ride one and she had thought that perhaps she could persuade her father once he had finished his book to take her to Hungary.

Now incredibly part of Hungary had come to her and she knew that it was an event that she would not forget when she returned home.

She looked at the horses in considerable detail.

There was silence as the Prince waited for her to give him her verdict.

Finally she said,

"There are two horses which to my mind, although of course I may be wrong, are finer than the others."

"Show me which they are," the

Prince insisted.

She pointed them out and he laughed.

"I suppose I might have known," he said. "I was testing you just to make sure."

"You are testing me for what, Sire?" Yolisa asked innocently.

"To see if you would choose the two horses I would have chosen myself," he replied.

"And may I ride one of them?" Yolisa enquired.

"Whichever one you like," the Prince answered.

She chose one with a star on its forehead and again the Prince laughed.

"Why are you laughing at me again?" Yolisa asked.

"Because I knew that that was the one you would choose and I was right."

He did not wait for her to answer, but ordered the groom to have the horse saddled.

They then mounted and rode out of the stable.

It was by a different door to the one that appeared to be the main entrance and then Yolisa was aware that there were three men mounted on horses following behind them.

She did not have to ask the question because the Prince informed her,

"I am forced to take an escort with me, but they will keep well behind us and will not infringe on us in any way."

"Of course you have to be protected," Yolisa said. "I know that you are always in danger."

As they were now in the open air, she knew that they could speak freely.

The Prince waited until a gate had been opened for them and, after they had passed through it, they were on open ground.

"There are a great many things I want to say to you," he said, "but first of all I think that we should give our horses their heads and gallop some of the enthusiasm out of them so that they do not interrupt us."

Yolisa smiled and set her horse off at a gallop.

Then they were racing over the

level ground, which seemed to stretch away towards a distant horizon.

There she could see very high mountains with their peaks glistening in the morning sunshine.

The horse she was riding was straining to beat the horse ridden by the Prince and Yolisa realised that she was moving faster than she had ever done before.

It was very exhilarating.

She was aware that the Prince rode magnificently and seemed to be a part of his horse.

They must have ridden for well over a mile before the Prince pulled in his reins saying,

"Now we can relax and talk without being afraid of being overheard by anyone, unless the bees have long ears and will buzz what we say in a communiqué to The Third Section!"

Yolisa could not help giving a little laugh.

At the same time she said,

"You do realise that they are trying to take your country away from you."

"Of course I realise it," the Prince replied. "They have already played innumerable dirty tricks to create riots among my people and they try to stir up trouble in every possible way they can think of."

"But your people are loyal, Sire?"

"So I believe," the Prince answered, "and thank you for coming to my rescue at this moment. I just could not believe that Her Majesty the Queen would fail me."

"She has no wish to do so," Yolisa answered, "and, as you well know, Sire, Great Britain has done everything it can to prevent the Russians from gaining access to the Mediterranean."

"I know that," the Prince said, "but I cannot survive without the assistance of your country."

"That is why I am here," Yolisa replied. "But I am only a drop in the ocean and you need a great deal more than just me."

"A very beautiful and a perfect drop," the Prince said.

The way he was speaking made Yolisa blush and she turned her head away.

"You are just so beautiful," the Prince said. "When I first saw you I could not believe that you were real. In fact I thought that you had been sent to me by the Gods on Mount Olympus."

Yolisa then wanted to tell him that she thought he looked just like a God, but she knew that it would be too intimate.

Instead she said,

"Let's enjoy just being here while the Russians and everyone else are far behind."

She looked back as she spoke.

The three Officers who were escorting the Prince were still nearly half a mile away.

"Now tell me about yourself," the Prince suggested. "How can you be so incredibly beautiful and at the same time so clever."

"Do cross your fingers when you say that," Yolisa said, trying to speak lightly. "I may make some terrible mistake and then you will send me home in disgrace."

"It is something that I will never do," the Prince answered. "Do you not think it is strange, Yolisa, that we can read each other's thoughts and, as well as that, have the same feelings."

Yolisa looked away from him.

"Perhaps it is just a coincidence," she murmured.

The Prince gave a low laugh.

"You don't believe that," he said, "and nor do I. I know that last night when you went to bed you were trying to be sensible in telling yourself that you had imagined the whole scenario and that it had not happened."

"Just how can you know that," Yolisa asked him in astonishment.

"Simply because I was feeling just the same," he replied. "And if you were surprised at meeting me, I was just as surprised at meeting you."

He gave a little chuckle as he added,

"And I was expecting an intelligent but rather plain young Englishwoman, who would lecture me when she had the chance and tell me how inferior I am to the power of the Union Jack."

Yolisa laughed because she could

not help it.

At the same time she was acutely conscious of the Prince.

It was difficult not to look at him as if he was a magician who had hypnotised her.

"I know just what you are thinking," the Prince said quietly. "I also know, as you realise, that we have been looking for each other for a long time, perhaps through a great number of other lives."

He paused and his voice altered as he went on,

"Now incredibly we have met in the most unusual circumstances. But we have met each other and that is all that matters."

CHAPTER FIVE

Yolisa found it just impossible to find an answer to what the Prince had said.

He gazed at her for a long moment.

"Let's ride on a little further," he suggested, "and then we must go back to civilisation."

The horses were only too willing and they rode on until it was easy to see the tall mountains ahead, some of which still had their cover of winter snow.

There was a stream running beneath them and, as they pulled in their horses near to it, Yolisa exclaimed,

"Your country is so lovely! Whatever happens, you must not lose it."

"That is what I keep saying to myself," the Prince replied, "but I am well aware that it will not be easy."

There was almost a sad note of despondency in his voice.

Without really thinking Yolisa said,

"You will win, I feel sure that you will win."

"Do you really mean that?" the Prince asked. "Or are you just trying to cheer me up?"

"You well know," Yolisa replied,

"that it would be impossible for me to lie to you."

He grinned.

"Yes, I know that."

"Then believe me when I say that every instinct I have ever had tells me that you will be triumphant, even though you have had to fight for what you now own."

The Prince smiled at her.

Then, when he was about to reply, he realised that the three Officers, who had been following them, were now drawing near.

Impatiently, as if he resented being interrupted, the Prince turned and faced them.

"What is it?" he asked sharply.

"I think, Your Royal Highness," one of the Officers answered, "we should turn back. You have an important conference with the Cabinet in two hours' time."

"I had forgotten," the Prince replied. "Very well! Her Ladyship and I will ride ahead and you can follow."

He set off with Yolisa and she realised that the Officers were waiting until they were some distance from them.

She could well understand the Prince's resentment at always having to be followed by a protective escort, but it was essential.

He must not suffer too the dreadful fate that Prince Alexander of Battenburg had endured at the hands of the Russians some years earlier.

They rode on very swiftly without speaking to each other.

Only when the Palace came into sight, gleaming white in the sunshine, did Yolisa say,

"Thank you very much, Sire, for what has been a most delightful and exciting ride."

"It is something we will do again and again," the Prince answered, "as long as Fate and our enemies allow us to do so."

"So what will we be doing this afternoon?" Yolisa enquired.

"We are making a great fuss about your arrival by having a Parade in the City Square as a special tribute to Queen Victoria."

He smiled a little mockingly as he added,

"As Her Majesty's Representative, although we do not say so openly, you will accept on her behalf the gold statue that Kavalla is presenting to her on the occasion of her Golden Jubilee."

Yolisa chuckled.

"I will try to look Royal, but I warn you that I am a very amateur actress."

"I think that you have done splendidly so far," the Prince said, "and since you look like Aphrodite, who could possibly challenge your antecedents?"

Yolisa laughed again and she felt a warmth within her heart.

He thought her to be as beautiful as Aphrodite, the Goddess of Love.

"Tomorrow morning," the Prince

went on, "we will ride off in a different direction to where there is situated an ancient Temple which is very like those that once stood at Delphi."

Yolisa's eyes lit up.

"I would love to see it," she said. "Please, please don't forget to take me there."

"I find it impossible to forget anything for you or about you," the Prince replied.

There was a note in his voice that made Yolisa feel shy.

But, as they rode on in silence, she told herself that she was now playing a really dangerous game.

'He is so attractive and so charming,' she thought, 'it would be impossible for any woman not to be entranced by him.'

It was even more difficult for her because she had met so few men and only in her dreams had there been anyone who in any way resembled the Prince.

They drew nearer to the Palace.

And when they had almost reached it, the Prince turned to her and said,

"You may not realise it yet, Yolisa, but you have encouraged and inspired me. I know now what I want and what I intend to have."

"I told you that you would win," Yolisa said. "Of course there will be many difficulties on the way, but you will overcome them all."

"As long as you help me, I know that is what I will do."

There was no chance of saying anything further as they had reached the gates and the sentries were saluting.

They rode to the Palace stable from where they had started out and there were grooms hurrying to the horses' heads.

Yolisa would have slipped from her saddle without any difficulty, but the Prince was too quick for her.

He dismounted from his horse rapidly and, while she was still putting down her reins, he waited to lift her to the ground.

For a moment Yolisa hesitated.

Then, as he reached up to put his hands round her small waist, she felt him draw her towards him.

Just for a moment he held her tightly before he set her down on the ground.

He gazed into her eyes as he did so.

And she felt again that strange feeling in her heart, while at the same time her whole body was vibrating to his body.

Then without speaking a word, they walked into the Palace.

Yolisa went upstairs and the Prince went away in another direction.

When she reached her bedroom, Yolisa felt as if she had come back to reality from a dream.

It had been so poignant, but at the very same time so thrilling that it could not really have happened.

Yet it had.

Yolisa knew now, because of what she had felt and what she and the Prince had said to each other that life could never be the same.

When she rang the bell, the maids came hurrying to assist her out of her riding clothes.

They helped her choose the elaborate gown she was to wear for the celebrations which were to take place later in the morning.

But first breakfast was waiting for her all laid out in her boudoir.

She had expected that she would have it downstairs with Lady Saville and the Colonel and perhaps also with some members of the Royal Household.

To her delight when she entered

the boudoir she found only her uncle waiting for her.

"Good morning, Uncle Harold!" she exclaimed at once. "It is delightful to find you here."

"You are late," he replied, "and I suppose you have a very good excuse for it."

Yolisa knew by the way he spoke and the look in his eyes that he was teasing her.

"You know where I have been," she said.

"Yes, I know," he answered. "And, of course, as your chaperone I very much disapprove, but then for other reasons that we will not mention here I am so pleased that you had the opportunity."

Yolisa sat down at the breakfast

table.

Two footmen brought in some delicious dishes and then withdrew.

"Did you enjoy yourself?" Lord Langford asked her when they were alone.

"It was wonderful, absolutely wonderful," Yolisa replied.

She could not help there being a rapt note in her voice.

Her uncle looked at her sharply before he said,

"Now you are worrying me. If what I suspect has happened, it could, my dearest child, eventually make you very unhappy."

"I realise that," Yolisa answered. "But everything is so different from what I expected."

She felt that she could not explain

it clearly.

As if Lord Langford did not want to worry her, he began to talk of the Parade that she was to attend.

"It was the Prince's idea," he began, "and a very clever one. It will show those who are watching us how attached this country is to Great Britain and that you have a special connection with the Queen."

"The Prince told me that I was to accept the gold statue that Kavalla is giving to Her Majesty."

"Again it was the Prince's idea," Lord Langford said, "and I think that he is a very intelligent young man. It would be a disaster if he could not make this country, as he most sincerely wants to do, an example for the rest of the Balkan States."

Yolisa was well aware of what he meant without him saying anything more.

He was obviously referring to the way that they had been overrun and had become nothing but slaves to their Russian Masters.

She knew, however, that, safe though they thought they were from any prying ears or eyes in this part of the Palace, it would be a mistake to take any chances.

She therefore replied to her uncle,

"I am sure that the Prince will achieve his ambition and Kavalla will be a shining example of new ideas and modern techniques, which are being developed in so many countries all over the world."

"Especially in America," Lord Langford added. "I intend to visit that country again very shortly. I think you would find it interesting to come along with me."

"That is a very kind and most generous offer, Uncle Harold," Yolisa smiled.

She realised as she spoke that Lord Langford was trying to attract her attention away from the Prince. He was also making it clear that when they left Kavalla she would have other interests to occupy her mind.

'If he thinks,' she said to herself, 'I can ever forget the Prince, he is wrong. Wherever I am and wherever I go, I shall always feel as if I have left some part of me behind in Kavalla.'

Even as the thought passed through her mind, she felt how ridiculous she was being.

She had met the Prince only yesterday.

How could she possibly feel like this about him so soon?

'I am behaving like a silly schoolgirl,' she thought, 'falling in love with the first handsome man I meet.'

Equally she knew that the Prince had spoken with an unmistakable sincerity.

The response from within herself had come from her heart and her soul.

Then she was aware that her uncle

was watching her and there was a worried expression in his eyes.

"I have made a mistake," he declared quietly, "in bringing you here. I can only hope that it is not something you will deeply regret in the future."

Yolisa put out her hand towards him.

"Whatever happens," she said, "I will never regret coming here or cease to be grateful to you for bringing me to Kavalla."

Lord Langford rose from the table.

"I am going now," he said, "to get ready for what lies ahead of us. I will collect you in about half an hour's time and I suggest you relax, or better still, write a letter to your father."

"I will do that and thank you again, Uncle Harold, for looking after me and being so kind."

"I feel that I have not succeeded in carrying out the former duty and it is impossible not to be kind to anyone as charming and beautiful as you."

He stopped for a moment before he added,

"Unfortunately there are other men who feel just the same."

Yolisa realised that he was referring to the Prince and, because it was in her mind, she could not help herself asking,

"I suppose that there have been a great number of beautiful women in his life."

"Of course," Lord Langford replied. "There has been a very beautiful and sinuous young woman staying at the Palace and I suspect that she was introduced by those people it is a mistake to name."

Yolisa's eyes widened.

"Do you really think that the Prince was deceived by her?"

"Not for a moment. He is far too clever for that and I doubt whether when their liaison ended she carried away anything of importance except her broken heart."

Yolisa thought that it was what she might well have deserved.

Of course the Russians would have tried to seduce the Prince and they had sent him one of their spies who was beautiful and alluring.

She would also have been experienced in extracting the information they required.

Yet because the Prince had a *Third Eye,* he would have known from the very beginning that the woman was dangerous.

Instead of being infatuated by her to the point of being indiscreet and easily manipulated, it was he who had captured her.

She had lost her heart to him and might even have forgotten that it was her duty to work on behalf of another nation hostile to Kavalla.

Yolisa with her creative imagination could almost see it all happening.

If there had been one woman sent to the Palace as bait by the Russians, there would doubtless be others.

Yet he had survived so far.

Now Yolisa had to help the Prince until the bride who had been chosen for him by Queen Victoria was old enough to take her place.

The mere thought of having to leave eventually was like the stab of a dagger in her heart.

Then because it seemed so absurd Yolisa wanted to laugh.

How was it possible that she could feel like this after meeting the Prince just three times in the last twenty-four hours?

It was only possible if what he had said was true and they really had been searching for each other for a long time in many other lives.

And now, past all belief, they had found each other!

It all circulated through Yolisa's mind.

As if he knew that there was nothing more he could say, Lord Langford walked towards the door.

"If you are writing to your father," he said as he reached it, "tell him that we may with luck return sooner than we expected."

Before Yolisa could reply he went out shutting the door somewhat sharply behind him.

She realised that he was annoyed.

Not particularly with her, Yolisa, but because the circumstances they now found themselves in were different from what he had envisaged at the outset.

She felt it was unlikely that he would take her away and yet that was what he was threatening to do.

'Then I will not go,' she told herself.

Equally she knew that it would be very difficult to refuse if her uncle insisted.

Yolisa next sat down at the writing table in front of the window and started a letter to her father.

Then, as she paused for words, she began to draw a picture of the Prince on a sheet of writing paper.

She was remarkably skilful in portraying his square forehead with his dark hair brushed back from it.

She drew his classical features and dark eyes.

And they seemed, when she

looked into them, to pierce their way into her very soul.

How could this have happened?

How could it be true?

Yet it was the most wonderful thing that could ever have happened to her!

She knew, if she could spend even a little time with the Prince, it would be a marvellous experience she would always remember.

It would enrich her whole life.

Later Yolisa went downstairs with Lord Langford.

And those who were waiting for them in the hall seemed to glitter.

The red coats of the Officers, the decorations and gold braid of those in authority and the gowns of the ladies were a panoramic kaleidoscope of intense colour.

Yolisa's dress was the blue of the summer sky and her hat was trimmed with little ostrich feathers in the same colour, which fluttered in the breeze.

She was wearing lovely jewellery that would have enhanced any gown however plain it was. It made hers seem even more glamorous.

Lord Langford had once given his wife a Christmas present of the most beautiful set of turquoises covered with diamonds.

There was a small collet for her neck and a large brooch to wear on her shoulder and bracelets, rings and earrings to complete the collection.

Yolisa was well aware that other

women looked at her with envy.

There was an expression in the Prince's eyes that she did not dare to translate.

He arrived after everyone waiting for him had been talking for nearly ten minutes.

When he did finally appear, the ladies sank in deep curtseys like the waves of the sea.

His Royal Highness was most certainly dressed for the part. He was wearing a white uniform coat, which was massed with decorations and he carried a feathered hat in his hand.

When he put it on his head, it made him look even more handsome than before.

As he had planned before she had

arrived, Yolisa travelled with him in the Royal carriage with both Lord Langford and the Prime Minister.

There was a procession of eight open carriages, all escorted by two troops of Cavalry and their rather dashing uniform was, Yolisa thought, very appealing.

The people of the City had been lining the streets since early in the morning and the moment the first horses appeared they began to cheer.

The children waved flags, which had been given to them by their schools.

'Only the Prince,' Yolisa thought to herself, 'could have thought of anything so clever as to distribute Union Jacks as well as the flag of

Kavalla.'

The two flags were also flying from the houses and the Cathedral.

'It will,' she added, 'convince the Russians better than anything else how strongly affiliated Kavalla is with the British Empire.'

Sitting next to the Prince, she felt that he looked very much a Ruler of his people.

They not only respected but loved him and there was no pretence about the cheers that rang out or the smiles of satisfaction on the faces of the Kavalleans.

Yolisa well knew that she would have been aware instinctively if there had been anything insincere about their behaviour.

She could feel that they reached

out to him as they passed by.

And, when he then appeared on the platform in the Square, the cheers were spontaneous.

The platform was crowded, but even so it was too small to hold all the Cabinet and the other dignitaries who had been invited to attend.

They were therefore seated on different platforms so that they could all be seen by the people.

Right in the centre of the Square there was a very impressive statue of a previous Ruling Prince.

Near to it there was a smaller statue covered by the combined flags of Kavalla and Great Britain.

Yolisa looked at it curiously.

As if the Prince knew at once that she was asking a question, he said,

"That is what I am going to unveil and then present to you the gold statue, which you will accept on behalf of Queen Victoria."

"I think you are very clever, Sire, to have planned all this," Yolisa said in a low voice.

"How do you know I planned — ?" he began.

Then he stopped and gave a laugh.

"That is a silly question, of course you would know even if no one had told you!"

"I still believe that it's very clever of Your Royal Highness," Yolisa persisted.

She could only speak to the Prince in a whisper as the Prime Minister had already risen to his feet.

He was telling the people why they had been asked to come here and why it was very important to Kavalla to have the close friendship of Great Britain and her powerful Monarch who had reigned for fifty years.

He spoke clearly and the people listened attentively to every word he said.

Then, when the Prince rose to his feet, the cheers broke out again.

As the women waved their handkerchiefs and the men their hats, Yolisa thought that it was very touching.

Only when the Prince held up his hand was there complete silence and he then told them briefly what great admiration he held for Queen Victoria.

And how they were honoured in having as their guest today, Lord Langford, who had a great affection for their country.

He had brought with him his niece, Lady Yolisa Ford, especially to represent Her Majesty the Queen on this auspicious occasion.

As he spoke, Yolisa saw some of the women and one or two politicians look at each other with surprise.

They were obviously finding it hard to understand why someone so young and of no particular importance should be Queen Victoria's representative.

As soon as the Prince had finished

speaking, he was escorted down into the centre of the Square.

Then, as he reached the covered statue, he started to speak again.

He explained how he had considered what would best represent the British Empire and its achievements over the world.

He had finally decided that nothing could be more appropriate than a statue of St. George killing the dragon.

As he spoke, it was obviously an innuendo pointed at the Russian menace.

Yolisa wondered if his speech was too dangerous, but at the same time it obviously appealed to the crowd.

As the Prince swept the cover off

the statue, they cheered and cheered again.

It was, Yolisa could see, very cleverly constructed as only, she thought, a Greek Sculptor could achieve.

Mounted on his horse St. George was piercing with his sword the dragon snarling beneath him, while his horse was rearing up.

Then the Prince once again held up his hand for silence.

He explained that this statue commemorated Queen Victoria's Jubilee and they were sending it her as a special present from Kavalla with their love and respect.

He was now asking their distinguished guest, Lady Yolisa Ford, to give it in person to the Queen when she returned to London.

There were cheers again as Yolisa walked slowly down from the platform to join the Prince.

She knew, as she did so, that he was watching her intently.

She almost felt as if his eyes pierced through her body to her heart.

When she reached him, she curtseyed.

Then they turned round to face the crowd before they walked side by side back to the platform.

Once again they stood together and then the people cheered and cheered.

Finally the band that had played before their arrival broke into first the National Anthem of Kavalla and then *God save the Queen.*

It was, of course, completely un-known to most of the Kavalleans.

It had been sung for them by the choir from the Cathedral and most of them pronounced the English words a little strangely.

They had, however, obviously taken great trouble in learning it and Yolisa thought it very moving.

Only when the music died away did the Prince say a few more words to the people.

"Since I became your Ruler," he said, "we have introduced many new ideas in this country, but there is a great deal more for us to do. I am determined that we shall be prosperous and at the same time peaceful and friendly with our neighbours."

Then there were murmurs, as if a number of the audience thought that it was impossible.

"This can only happen," the Prince went on, "if we are united in ourselves and determined to make Kavalla an independent and respected country. I believe that if we all strive together that this, with God's blessing, is what we can easily achieve."

He spoke with such a note of sincerity that Yolisa felt the tears come into her eyes.

Then, as he finished, he looked at her and she knew that he was aware of what she felt and was moved by his words.

There were a great many people

for the Prince to speak to and to introduce to Yolisa, but she was well aware that they thought it very unusual that he should make so much fuss about her.

"He could not do more," she heard one woman say, "if it was his bride-to-be who was with him."

They then moved amongst the Statesmen and other dignitaries, but the crowd had no intention of dispersing and stood still watching them intently.

The band was now playing spirited national songs that were known to them all.

They therefore started to sing, their voices soaring up in the sunshine.

The colourful dresses of the

women, the fluttering flags and the uniforms of the soldiers made an arresting picture.

It was, Yolisa thought, what any artist would like to paint.

It all took quite a long time and it was after one o'clock before they finally drove back to the Palace.

There were still people lining the route, who waved frantically as they passed.

The Prince saluted and Yolisa raised her hand in an energetic wave.

She knew that it was what the Queen would have done had she been in her place.

When finally they did reach the Palace, the Prince said,

"You were really wonderful, Lady

Yolisa. I can only congratulate you on —"

He was just about to add,

"Appearing more Royal than Royalty," when he realised that the Prime Minister was still with them, who was not aware of the parts they were acting to deceive the Russians.

Hastily Lord Langford piped up,

"Excellent, absolutely excellent, Yolisa. I am quite sure that Her Majesty will be very gratified at the beautiful present Kavalla has given her."

"I hope so as well," the Prime Minister said, "and that Lady Yolisa will tell Her Majesty just how much we admire both her and the British Empire."

"I will certainly do so," Yolisa replied.

"When are you thinking of returning to England?" the Prime Minister asked her.

It was an awkward question and, as Yolisa glanced to her uncle for help, the Prince said,

"Come along now, what we all need is a glass of champagne and, if your throat is not dry, Prime Minister, mine certainly is."

The Prime Minister laughed.

"I would definitely appreciate a glass, Your Royal Highness."

"Then what are we waiting for?" the Prince asked as the carriage came to a standstill.

He stepped out and helped Yolisa to alight.

As he did so, he whispered beneath his breath,

"You were just perfect, but then you could never be anything else."

Yolisa felt herself give a little quiver.

She was thinking as she did so that his performance had been no less perfect than hers.

The people who were invited to luncheon filled the Banqueting Hall. They even spilled into the passage where the *aides-de-camp* were obliged to sit since there was no other room for them.

Everyone was in a very good humour and delighted that the unveiling of the statue had gone off so well.

But Yolisa knew that some of the

Councillors had been somewhat critical.

They had been afraid, although they did not dare to say so, that it might annoy the Russians.

In which case they would undoubtedly find some excuse for interfering even more than they had been doing already.

Several members of the Cabinet told Lord Langford about the many difficulties and problems the Russians set for them and that they were aware that infiltration into the country was increasing.

But they had no notion of how to prevent it.

"Our one comfort," one Councillor suggested, "is that His Royal Highness has expanded the Army and they are all wholeheartedly loyal to him."

"I do hope you are certain of that," Lord Langford said. "It was, as you know, the hostility of the Bulgarian Army that eventually caused Prince Alexander to abdicate after the Russians had been obliged to return him to his own country."

"I well remember it," the Councillor replied. "At the same time I can assure you that our Army is totally at the service of Prince Nikos."

"That is what I hoped to hear," Lord Langford said.

When luncheon was finished the guests lingered for a little while longer.

Some walked on the terrace outside the front of the Palace to look down at the huge crowds, which were still congregating in the streets below.

The fountains were playing and the flowers seemed to be even more colourful than they had the day before and Yolisa thought it must be the most beautiful Royal Palace in the world.

Because the crowds saw them looking down, they started to cheer.

Finally the Prime Minister proposed to the Prince,

"I think that Your Royal Highness should appear and perhaps say just a few words to them. They have been waiting there since early this morning."

"I am aware of that," the Prince

said, "and I think it would also please them, because I doubt if they were in the Square, to meet Lady Yolisa."

He did not wait for the Prime Minister's reply.

Going up to Yolisa, he took her by the hand.

"Come down and meet my people," he said. "I want them to know you."

Yolisa had not heard what the Prime Minister said and she was surprised.

Then, as the Prince started to draw her down the steps, she asked so that only he could hear,

"Is it wise? There are many people today who have doubted that I was important enough to accept your present for Queen Victoria. And they will certainly question my appearing with you alone."

"You are my Guest of Honour," the Prince replied, "and, of course, as you do know, the Goddess I have been seeking for a very long time."

Yolisa drew in her breath.

There was nothing she could say.

As they then reached the last few steps, the Prince stopped.

By now the people in the street realised what was happening and had rushed forward.

They pressed themselves against the iron railings where there were two sentries on duty.

It was easy for the crowd to see the Prince clearly and Yolisa standing beside him. They were clearly excited that he had come down to them and eager to hear what he had to say.

When the Prince held up his hand for silence, they instantaneously stopped cheering.

He thanked them for showing such an interest in this important day and he told them, as he had done in the Square, how Kavalla was sending a very special present to Queen Victoria on her Golden Jubilee.

Then he said,

"This present is being taken to London by our very special English guest, who we welcome not only because she is a representative of Queen Victoria but because she is in fact the most beautiful woman in the world!"

As he spoke, Yolisa gave a little gasp and looked at him in astonishment.

The crowd was delighted and cheered loudly before the Prince added,

"As you know, I am Greek by birth and to me the most superb of the Goddesses is Aphrodite, the Goddess of Love. Love is what I think we in Kavalla can give to the world, which is in such constant trouble with one country fighting against another."

He paused for a moment and then went on,

"Let's see if we can have here in our own beautiful land the special love that is identified with that

Goddess and believe that just as we are sending a present to Queen Victoria, she has sent us a sublime representative in Lady Yolisa."

As he finished speaking, he lifted Yolisa's hand to his lips and, as she quickly curtseyed, he kissed it.

The crowd was delighted.

They cheered and shouted until at last the Prince turned round.

Offering Yolisa his arm, he walked slowly up the steps.

Halfway up they stopped to wave to those cheering below and again when they reached the top step.

Only as she saw the expressions on the faces of those guests who had heard what the Prince had said did Yolisa feel embarrassed.

It was, however, impossible for

her to say anything.

With a sense of relief she realised that in order to be rid of his guests the Prince was now retiring.

He did not say farewell to anyone except the Prime Minister.

He just walked off the terrace and into the Palace and disappeared.

Yolisa looked for her uncle.

When he came towards her, they too slipped away from the other guests and went up to their rooms.

"All I can say," Lord Langford said when they were alone on the wide landing, "is that the Prince has a very good sense of the romantic!"

"I had no idea he would say anything like that," Yolisa murmured.

"Nor did anyone else," her uncle

replied. "They were all astonished and I daresay that a great number of the ladies present are ready to scratch your eyes out!"

Yolisa laughed.

"I hope they will not do that, at least not until after I have left."

"That is another question we have to answer," Lord Langford said.

"Surely we cannot leave," Yolisa suggested, "until Her Majesty can name the Princess to whom the Prince will be betrothed."

"I realise that, Yolisa. At the same time I cannot allow you to be embroiled in or shall I say bemused and even besotted by what is happening here."

"We have to help him, Uncle Harold, *we have to*!" she cried.

"I know, but I have a feeling that he is moving too fast. As you have just pointed out, there may well be a long wait before a British Princess can sit beside him on the Throne."

Yolisa did not answer, but gave a deep sigh.

She knew, whatever fears her uncle might have, they would both of them strive in every way possible to prevent Kavalla being overrun by the Russians.

How could they allow the Prince to be deposed in favour of some puppet who would be put in his place?

"I think, Uncle Harold," she said aloud, "we just have to pray that things will work out for the best. One thing is obvious, the people of

Kavalla love their Prince."

"I realise that and perhaps as you hope, my dearest, we shall win the battle that lies before us. But it is not going to be easy!"

CHAPTER SIX

Yolisa woke with a start.

For a brief moment she could not think what was happening.

Then she realised that she was in bed and had been asleep.

Before she had retired to bed she had pulled back the curtains so that she could see the stars.

The brilliant moonshine was pouring in through the windows turning everything into silver.

She stared at it for a moment.

Then she was aware that it had

been a voice that had called her.

She knew, almost as if someone had told her, that the Prince was in danger.

Without considering or thinking of what she should do, she jumped out of bed.

She went towards the door leading into the corridor and then stopped.

She could hardly go to the Prince's State Apartment wearing only her nightgown.

On the *chaise longue* by the dressing table were her underclothes for the next day, arranged neatly by the maid who had helped her to undress.

It took her only a few seconds to slip them on and she then ran to the wardrobe and took down the first gown her hand touched.

It fastened down the front.

She was still doing up the buttons when she crossed the room again towards the door.

Only then did she wonder if she would be able to see her way.

She pulled the door open.

Then, as she started almost to run, a door at the far end of the corridor opened.

It then flashed through her mind that it might be a servant who would ask her where she was going.

She came to a standstill.

Then to her relief she saw that it was the Prince and he was holding a lantern in his hand.

She ran towards him.

"You are in danger!" she called out. "I was coming to warn you. You must hide somewhere!"

"I was just coming to tell you the same thing," the Prince replied.

He spoke in a very low voice and, as if he had told her to be silent, Yolisa did not reply.

He put out his hand and took hers.

Turning round, he walked through the door of the boudoir which he had just opened.

By the light of the lantern they crossed into another room, which was shut up with the curtains pulled for the night.

Then the Prince opened yet another door where the candles were still alight.

It was, Yolisa saw, his own bed-room.

The covers on the bed were thrown back.

He must have jumped out of the huge four-poster hung with red curtains in a hurry.

He did not say anything, but pulled Yolisa across the room.

They stopped abruptly in front of a panelled wall and for a long moment she did not understand what was happening.

Then the Prince put out his hand and touched a spring.

Slowly the panel opened.

The Prince went ahead of her carrying his lantern.

And Yolisa saw that there was a

narrow staircase descending straight down to the ground floor.

Having stepped forward, the Prince stopped for a moment to close the panelling behind Yolisa.

Still without speaking he walked slowly down the narrow staircase while she followed him.

She was to learn a long time later that the staircase had been built at the same time as the Palace itself and the reigning Prince in his old age liked a variety of women, who were not in any way connected with the Court.

The staircase was built so that they could visit him secretly and none of his staff were aware of their presence at any time.

Eventually people did find out

and whispered about this strange obsession and the women who came up the staircase were called 'the ladies of the night.'

The Prince and Yolisa now reached the bottom of the staircase.

There was a high narrow door in front of them, which was securely bolted.

The Prince drew back the bolts.

When Yolisa walked out, she found herself in the garden and she was concealed behind some bushes which were in blossom.

When she looked back, the Prince was closing the door they had just come through. It was so skilfully made that it was impossible to see that it was not part of the wall.

The Prince had blown out his

lantern and left it inside.

Again he took Yolisa's hand.

He drew her away from the Palace, but all the time they kept moving through the bushes.

On one side of them was the lawn
with a fountain in the middle of it,
which was smaller than those in the
front of the Palace, but no less
beautiful.

It had a delightful carved basin,
which portrayed cupids and doves.
The water being thrown up towards
the sky in the moonlight was very
lovely.

Yolisa would have liked to stop
and look at it.

But she was aware that the Prince
was in a great hurry.

She sensed danger as he did.

All the time since leaving her bedroom she could feel that the danger was coming nearer to him.

She was sure that he felt the same.

They twisted and turned through the rhododendrons and lilacs and then they reached the trees which grew at the back of the Palace, which Yolisa had admired when she arrived.

It was then that the Prince stopped.

He stood gazing to the right as if he was expecting to see someone.

Yolisa looked back through the trees towards the fountain to have a last glimpse of it.

Then she gave out a little gasp and clutched at the Prince.

He turned towards her and, as he

did so, saw what she had seen.

Coming through a clump of trees, which were very like those they were sheltering under, were two men.

Instinctively Yolisa knew that they were enemies.

She moved closer to the Prince.

He put his arm round her and pulled her nearer to the trunk of a tree.

They were almost behind it, although they could still see the two men.

They stood for some minutes looking towards the Palace.

It was as if they were searching for a sign of anyone awake or perhaps just a light in one of the windows.

Then one of the men turned round and beckoned and they were joined immediately by several other men.

Then, as the first two started to move, still more appeared from the wood behind them.

There must have been well over a dozen now as they crept across the lawn.

They were bending their bodies as if they hoped to be less conspicuous and Yolisa thought that they carried weapons in their hands.

Although she was terrified, it was impossible not to go on watching them as they drew nearer and nearer to the Palace.

They moved directly towards the part that she and the Prince had just left, where his Private Apartments were located.

It was so eerie and frightening that she found it almost impossible to breathe. She could only watch the intruders as if mesmerised.

They were moving very silently.

It was not possible to hear anything but the soft drip of the water from the fountain.

Then, as they reached the Palace, Yolisa saw them stop in front of a side door.

One which Yolisa thought was perhaps used only by the Prince when he wanted to go into the garden alone at night.

The men, and now there was no doubt that they were armed, had stopped.

Yolisa wondered if they would force the door in some manner to obtain entry.

Then to her surprise, without their having made a sound, the door opened.

She knew at once that it must be a Russian Agent inside the Palace who was letting them in.

There were only two sentries guarding the Royal Apartments and they would be powerless to prevent the Russians from kidnapping the Prince as they obviously intended to do.

They would abduct him and keep him a prisoner in Russian hands and no one would know exactly what had happened to him.

The Prince, who was watching

intently like Yolisa, had not moved.

But she sensed that he had stiffened when the door opened.

She thought that it was humiliating for him to think that at least one of his people in his Palace was a Russian spy.

Then, as the last men went slowly through the door, it was closed.

It all happened so quickly and silently that Yolisa felt that what she had just seen must be a figment of her imagination.

Yet she knew that the Prince's instinct and hers had saved him from the Russians and it had been with only a few seconds to spare.

Impulsively she turned towards him.

In sheer relief she hid her face

against his shoulder.

For a moment he held her very close to him and she thought that his heart was beating as fast as hers.

Still without speaking he took her hand and started to move through the trees behind them.

Yolisa wondered where they were going.

She was afraid that when the Russians could not find the Prince in his bedroom they would begin to search for him elsewhere.

The trees seemed to thicken a little and then they came to a clearing in the centre of which there was a small pool.

On the other side of it Yolisa saw there were two horses held by a young man.

She knew, as the Prince hurried towards them, that he had expected to find them there.

When they reached the horses, Yolisa saw that the boy holding them was small and dark and quite obviously Greek.

As the Prince saw him, he said, and it was the first time he had spoken,

"Thank you, Ajax. I knew you would not fail me. You were only just in time."

"The Gods were with us," Ajax said answering in Greek.

The Prince then picked up Yolisa and set her on the saddle of one of the horses.

She saw that it was a side-saddle and realised that the Prince must have been certain that she would be going with him.

He mounted the other horse.

"Warn the guard, Ajax," he said. "At the same time be very careful you are not seen or that anyone else realises that you have informed them."

"Don't worry, Master," Ajax replied.

He gave a salute as the Prince turned his horse to go deeper into the wood.

Yolisa followed him and they were obliged to ride in single file.

It was quite a long time before they emerged from the trees onto open ground.

Now at last, Yolisa thought, she would be able to speak to the

Prince.

But to her surprise he pushed his horse forward into a gallop and she had to do the same to keep up with him.

It was only then that she realised with a shock that she was most inappropriately dressed for riding.

She had taken the first gown that her hand touched in the wardrobe. It was a very pretty one of white muslin with a wide frilled skirt and round her small waist was a sash of blue satin.

It was a dress that Yolisa thought she would have worn for an important social occasion.

Now her hair was falling over her shoulders and she feared that the Prince must think she looked very strange.

Only when they had ridden for what seemed quite a long way did he go a little slower.

Yolisa was now able to ride side by side with him.

"We are very lucky to have escaped," he said. "If you had not been dressed and ready for me when I came for you, we might have been too late."

"I realise that," Yolisa said, "but I woke with a start and felt very strongly that someone was telling me that you were in danger."

"And so you were coming to save me," the Prince said quietly.

"How could anyone have guessed or imagined that the Russians would strike so quickly?" Yolisa exclaimed.

"I think," the Prince said, "perhaps we rather overdid our affection and respect for your Queen and they then thought that they could rid the country of me before I was actually married to a bride of Her Majesty's choice."

"But what will happen now?" Yolisa asked in a small frightened voice.

"That," he replied firmly, "is in the lap of the Gods."

As if he had no wish to say anything more, he hurried forward.

Once again they were riding swiftly, although where they were going Yolisa had no idea.

Just in front of them was another long wood and it seemed to stretch out along the coastline with the sea on their right.

The Prince entered the wood ahead of Yolisa.

There was a mossy path twisting among the trees and they were obliged to ride again in single file.

Then suddenly, in what Yolisa thought must be the very centre of the wood, she saw a roof.

It was so unexpected that she thought perhaps it was just the trick of the moonlight.

As they moved further on and the trees thinned, she saw in front of her that there was a Church.

It was only a small Church, which appeared to be built of wood. There was a cross over the doorway and steps up to a large oak door.

As the Prince dismounted, a boy came running from the side of the Church to go to his horse's head.

The Prince turned towards Yolisa and he lifted her down from the saddle.

His hands were on her waist and he held her close to him as he did so.

She looked at him and was about to speak when she saw that the Church door had now opened and an elderly Priest was standing on the top of the steps.

The Prince put Yolisa down beside him.

Taking her by the hand, he moved towards the Priest.

The boy, who was holding the bridle of his horse, took Yolisa's as well and then he led both the horses away into the trees.

The Prince walked the short distance to where the Priest was now standing at the bottom of the steps.

Then to Yolisa's surprise he went down on his knees in front of him.

"I have now come to you, Father," he said, "for your protection and help."

"I knew that," the Priest said in a deep voice, "and I was expecting you, my son."

He put his hand on the Prince's head as if he blessed him.

The Prince rose to his feet and said,

"Let me present Lady Yolisa Ford, who knew as you did that I was in danger."

"So she too hears the voice of God," the Priest smiled. "Now, my children, you are safe for the moment."

"We are very grateful, Father," the Prince said. "And it will make me very happy if you would *marry* us immediately."

Yolisa gave a little gasp of sheer amazement.

The Priest bowed and replied,

"It will give me great pleasure, my son. It will only take me a short while to be ready for you both."

"I will take Yolisa into the house," the Prince said.

Taking her hand, he drew her round the side of the Church.

She saw behind it that there was a small house. It also was built of wood and was very picturesque.

As they moved she was aware of small rabbits running ahead of them on the path and there were squirrels looking down at them from the trees.

The Prince opened the front door of the house and they walked into a small but attractive room.

There was a large fireplace, a few comfortable chairs and a large collection of books in shelves.

As the Prince took his hand from hers, Yolisa, who had been silent from sheer shock, murmured,

"How can you ask the Priest to marry us? You know I cannot marry you."

"But I intend to marry you," the Prince declared firmly.

"But you must not! You know that you have to marry Royalty! The bride Her Majesty has chosen for you will come to Kavalla — as soon as she is old enough."

The Prince made a wide gesture with his hands.

"In the meantime, my darling, I am a Prince without a Throne, escaping from an enemy that I have not been able to conquer. The only thing I have to offer you is my heart."

"I love you," Yolisa said. "Of course I love you. At the same time I cannot do anything so wrong as to let you marry me when I know that the only way you can save your country is by having the protection of England."

The Prince smiled.

"The Union Jack cannot protect me at the moment," he said. "The only people who I can really trust are you and my Guardian and Teacher, Father Stavros."

"So he taught you," Yolisa said, "and he has a *Third Eye* because he knew that you were coming to him."

"To him it is the voice of God. When I woke as you did and realised that danger was encroaching upon me, I was quite sure that Father Stavros would be expecting us."

"It is all very strange and wonderful," Yolisa sighed. "Equally please be sensible. You must not marry me."

"Yet you say you love me," the Prince said in a deep voice.

He moved a little nearer to her as he added,

"The moment I saw you I just knew that you were the woman I had been seeking all my life and in my dreams."

"I felt the same," Yolisa said, "but I fought against it because I knew that I would have to go back to England, though it would be impossible to forget you."

"I have no intention of allowing you to forget me. So, as soon as Father Stavros is ready for us, we will be married. Whatever happens in the future, at least we will be together."

"It sounds too wonderful," Yolisa

murmured. "But I know that I should save you — from yourself."

The Prince chuckled.

"I have no wish to be saved. I want you, my darling, and you know, without my telling you, that you already belong to me. You are part of me just as I am part of you. It is quite impossible for us to live without each other."

"That is what I feel," Yolisa said in a very small voice. "At the same time everyone will be — very angry."

"So let them be. At the moment neither of us know what the future will hold. If the Russians take my country, then we shall have to sail away to some unknown destination. But we *will* be together."

"Please, please," Yolisa pleaded. "Let's wait for a little while and see what happens. Perhaps the Russians who were about to kidnap you will be taken prisoner and —"

"They will try again," the Prince interrupted her. "In fact again and again until somehow they succeed."

He paused for a moment before he went on,

"Of course I will try to prevent them from taking over the country. I will fight them with every weapon I have. At the same time I know that I cannot live without you. Just as I need you with my heart and my soul, so I need your mind and what you call your *Third Eye* to protect and inspire me."

"When you talk to me like that,"

Yolisa answered, "it's impossible for me to know — what is right and what is wrong."

"What is right is that you should follow what Father Stavros calls, 'the voice of God'," the Prince said firmly, "which will tell you that you belong to me."

Yolisa did not answer and after a moment he continued,

"Do you really think, my precious, that I can stay here alone with you and not make you mine? I have no wish to shock or frighten you, but you must understand that is what I might do, even if you have no Wedding ring on your finger."

"I love you, you know — how much I love you," Yolisa said breathlessly.

The Prince smiled.

"Father Stavros is waiting for us."

Yolisa put her hand up to her hair.

"How can I be married like this?" she asked.

"Very easily," the Prince replied. "The only onlookers to criticise you will be the squirrels and the birds of the forest, which are very attracted to Father Stavros, as they were to St. Francis and which worship as we will in the Church I built for him."

He looked down at Yolisa with an expression of love in his eyes that made her draw in her breath.

"No one," he said quietly, "could look more beautiful. I am prepared not only to love you, my exquisite perfect bride, but to worship you."

As the Prince finished speaking, he drew her across the room.

They went out through the front door of the little house and then walked back through the trees in silence.

They climbed up the stone steps into the Church.

While they had been away, Father Stavros had lit six candles on a table in front of the high screen and there were two large ones set on gold stands on either side of it.

The Church itself was very lovely.

It had been carved, Yolisa was to learn much later, by the loving hands of great craftsmen and their talent has been handed down from one generation to another in one special district of Kavalla.

Unlike most Churchs, the stained glass windows that were small, long and pointed, were open.

Coming in through them from the wood were birds and squirrels. They sat on the beams and windowsills and watched totally unafraid as the Prince then took Yolisa up the nave on his arm.

There were a great many wild flowers arranged on the table and in other parts of the small Church.

Yolisa was to learn later that they were brought as thank offerings by the children Father Stavros taught. Their parents were woodcutters and guardians of the woods.

Father Stavros was at the altar now wearing a beautiful embroidered vestment.

When the Prince and Yolisa stood in front of him, he began the Marriage Service.

He spoke very quietly and sincerely and Yolisa felt that she must listen to every word as the birds and squirrels seemed to be doing.

The moment came for the Priest to bless the ring.

The Prince took his signet ring from his little finger and, when it was blessed, placed it on Yolisa's third finger.

It was a small but very beautiful ring and she saw in the centre of it that there was an emerald which gleamed in the candlelight.

Then, when they knelt, Father Stavros blessed them.

As he did so, Yolisa knew that a

shaft of dazzling light encircled them.

The Blessing came not only from the Priest but from God Himself.

Then, as if to show that the Service was finished, Father Stavros went down on his knees in front of the altar.

The Prince drew Yolisa to her feet and, slipping her arm through his, they walked back to the door.

Yolisa was deeply moved by the Ceremony and by the light that she had seen encircle them both.

She felt that she could hear the angels singing and they had passed from this world into another.

The Prince took her through the trees back to the little house.

When he opened the door, he

went through the sitting room.

There was a small passage beyond it, which led, Yolisa found, to a bedroom.

"I built this for myself," the Prince said in a deep voice, "so that when I wanted to escape from the difficulties of the Throne I could come to Father Stavros for help."

He paused to look down at Yolisa and went on,

"Now I have come, as I have always wanted to, with someone I love, someone who belongs to me and who is mine for all Eternity."

As he finished speaking, he put his arms round Yolisa and kissed her very gently.

It was the first time he had done so, but she knew that it was what she had longed for.

She felt her heart leap towards him.

Every instinct in her body quivered as he touched her.

He held her captive for a long moment and then he said,

"I love you my precious adorable wife and I want to tell you how much. Get into bed and I will not be long."

Almost before Yolisa could realise just what was happening he took his arms from her.

He walked away out through another door leaving her alone.

For a moment she was so bewildered that she wanted to run after him.

Then she understood that this

was her bedroom and he was un-
dressing next door.

There was a candle burning on
one side of the bed and there was
no other light except for the moonlight which was streaming in
through the open window.

Hastily, because he had told her
what he wanted, Yolisa took off her
pretty white dress.

She thought now that it had been
almost appropriate as a bridal
gown.

There was a cupboard where she
could hang it up and then she took
off the other clothes which she had
put on so hastily in the Palace.

Suddenly she realised that she
had no nightgown.

She felt shy and at the same time

a little frightened.

She slipped into the bed.

As it was big, it took up most of the room.

There were fresh muslin curtains hanging from a small corolla at the back of it and the sheets and pillowcases, as in the Palace, were edged with lace.

This was the Prince's bed.

Now she was in it because she was his wife.

The whole world seemed to have turned upside down.

How was it possible that she was really married to the Prince whom she loved with all her heart and soul?

She knew that it was something she should not have done, yet it had been impossible to refuse him.

'I love him, *I love him,*' she said to herself over and over again.

She waited breathlessly.

The door on the other side of the room opened.

The Prince came in.

He was wearing a long robe of some dark material and he came to the bedside.

Yolisa thought that he would sit down on it and perhaps talk to her.

Instead he blew out the candles, took off his robe and got into bed.

He put out his arms and felt her trembling.

"My precious, my darling," he said, "you are not to be frightened. What we have done is, I know, what is right and good and I cannot allow you to regret for one moment that you are now my wife."

"I am not regretting it," Yolisa managed to whisper. "It is just that it seems like a wonderful dream that cannot possibly be true."

"I will make it true," the Prince asserted in a deep voice.

He drew her a little closer.

As he felt her quiver, he said,

"You are so lovely and so exquisite in every way that I am convinced you have come to me from Mount Olympus. I am only afraid that you will disappear and I shall have lost you."

"How could you ever love me?" Yolisa asked. "How is it possible that all this has happened so quickly?"

"As I told you before," he replied, "we have known each other for a million years and now I have found you I will never let you go as long as we live."

As he finished speaking, he kissed her.

Not gently as he had done before, but possessively, as if he wanted to be quite sure that she realised she was his.

To Yolisa it was as if the moonlight from outside swam through her body.

The stars twinkled in her breasts.

She felt that she was no longer on earth but floating in the sky above the bright blue sea.

As the Prince continued kissing her, his hands were touching her body.

Their hearts were beating against each other.

She felt an ecstasy that was beyond anything that she had ever known or imagined and she knew that the Prince felt the same.

The stars beyond the window became more insistent and the moonlight turned to the warmth of the sun.

As the Prince then made Yolisa his, they moved into a Heaven that was especially made for lovers.

Yolisa stirred and the Prince asked her,

"Are you awake, my darling?"

"How could I possibly sleep — when I am so happy?" she murmured. "I thought when you were loving me that if we died tonight we should have known everything that was perfect and had found a special Heaven all of our own."

"That is what I thought too," the Prince replied. "But I was afraid of hurting or frightening you."

"How could you do either when you have made me so happy? All I want to do is to make you happy too."

"How could you imagine that I am anything else?" the Prince asked. "I have been very lonely at times, my precious one. Even though I love the people I rule over and many of them I know love me, it's not the same as having someone who thinks and feels as I do. And of course loves as I do."

The last words were almost a question.

"I love you, I adore you," Yolisa sighed. "You will be tired of my telling you so — but I want to go on saying it over and over again."

"Which is just what I want you to do," the Prince said, "because it makes me not only the happiest man in the world but the luckiest."

"Do you think that — everyone will be very angry with us?" Yolisa asked in a low voice.

"If they are, what does it matter?" the Prince asked. "I have already warned you, my darling, that if Kavalla does not want me I shall be a wanderer of the earth without a Throne and with very little to offer you except myself."

"Do you think — I want anything else?" Yolisa replied. "Even if we are very poor I will look after you and our love will be even stronger that it is already — because we have to fight the world to survive."

The Prince was so touched by what she said that he could not answer her.

He just kissed her again.

Their hearts were both beating fiercely and they clung to each other as if the world was trying to pull them apart.

"You are mine, mine completely," he cried. "How could I have guessed that a tiresome young woman who was coming from England to pretend to be my future wife would be *you*?"

Yolisa gave a little laugh.

"It does seem absurd and I am afraid that Uncle Harold will be very angry."

"I don't think so," the Prince replied. "Your uncle is a very intelligent man and he may understand, where a great many other people would not, that we just cannot live without each other."

"That is true and I am just so happy to be with you that perhaps Uncle Harold and everyone else will forgive me."

"If they do not," the Prince added, "you will have to be content with me."

Yolisa put her arms round his neck and the Prince drew her close to him.

"All I want is — you," she whispered, "and, if the women of Kavalla think that I have stolen their Prince from them, there is nothing they can do about it."

"You have stolen me from no one," the Prince insisted, "and I know that there will never be any other woman in my life but you. How could there be when I have found utter perfection and no man could ask for more?"

There was no need for Yolisa to reply to him.

She could only let him kiss her and go on and on kissing her.

Once more they were flying towards the sky.

The world was left behind and

they were enveloped in the light and love of God.

CHAPTER SEVEN

Yolisa felt that she was in a dream Heaven.

She woke up in the morning, because the Prince was kissing her.

Later she found herself swimming beside him in the pool that was just a little way from the house.

It all seemed unreal and incredibly wonderful.

The pool was a surprise.

When the Prince had told Yolisa that was where they would go after breakfast, she exclaimed.

"But I have nothing to wear!"

He smiled and she asked,

"You don't mean — ?"

"No one will see you, my darling, but me," he answered, "and, as you look just like Aphrodite, clothes I can assure you are unimportant."

She thought that it was rather unfair.

He had bathing clothes which he had left with Father Stavros.

However, they walked from the house to the pool with Yolisa wearing his dark robe and the Prince had only a towel wrapped around his waist.

He was indeed quite right in saying that no one would see them.

There were only rabbits that ran ahead of them and the squirrels chattering in the trees.

Fish jumped out of their way as they plunged into the pool.

The water was cool and clear and Yolisa felt that it was a fairy pool especially made for them.

Afterwards they lay on the soft grass.

Although there was so much that they had to say to each other, it was easier to make love.

When they went back to the house, luncheon was laid for them in the sitting room.

Yolisa had learned that Father Stavros was looked after by the two pupils who were in his charge at the moment.

One of them was the son of an aristocratic Greek and the other was the son of a doctor who worked in the mountains at the far end of Kavalla.

They were both boys of fifteen and very intelligent and they had already decided that they would eventually enter the Priesthood.

However, Father Stavros was wise enough to say that they must not make the final decision for their future until they were very much older.

After the Prince and Yolisa had finished luncheon, he insisted that they rested in their bedroom.

She had no wish to argue with him.

She knew that they were both longing to be in that world where there were no troubles, no difficulties and no problems of any kind.

There was just love and love.

Every minute she loved the Prince more.

Later that evening they went to the little Church and the Prince knew that Father Stavros would be having his Evening Service.

"He may be alone or there may be someone there," he said, "but anyway they will not interfere with us nor will they let anyone in the City know where I am."

He spoke reassuringly.

At the same time Yolisa felt a little nervous.

It was a relief when they entered the Church to find that only the two students were kneeling beside Father Stavros at the altar.

There was no one else at all in the Church except the little creatures from the forest. They were peeping in through the windows or sitting on the wooden beams.

When the Service was over, the two students withdrew and the Prince then took Yolisa by the hand and drew her up to Father Stavros.

"You are happy, my children?" he asked them.

"Happier than we could ever put into words," the Prince replied. "God has blessed us and we have found the love which He gives to those who believe in Him."

"That is just what I want you to feel, my son," Father Stavros replied.

They knelt before him and he

blessed them both again.

They then left him to his prayers and went back to the little house.

It was the next morning before Yolisa began to wonder what was happening in the City.

Were the Russians searching for the Prince?

"Should we try to find out what is going on?" she asked him a little nervously.

"I expect we shall know soon enough," he answered. "But for the moment I have no feeling of danger."

"Nor have I," Yolisa agreed with him. "At the same time, my wonderful husband, I just cannot help being afraid for you."

She moved closer to him as she spoke and he put his arms around her.

"Whatever happens now or in the future," he said, "we are together and nothing else is of any consequence."

He spoke very positively and he then refused to talk any more about the difficulties that lay ahead.

All the same, because she was afraid for him, Yolisa could not help worrying.

It was nearly time for luncheon when they came back from the pool.

They had just finished dressing when the front door of the house opened.

To Yolisa's astonishment Lord

Langford walked in.

"Uncle Harold!" she exclaimed.

The Prince, who was pouring out a glass of wine, turned round.

"I thought, my Lord, that you would find us sooner or later," he said.

"I knew this is where you would be," Lord Langford said, "before Ajax told me."

He kissed Yolisa on the cheek and said,

"If you have a glass of wine for me, I would appreciate it. It was very hot riding here through the woods and not being certain if I was going in the right direction."

"You came alone?" the Prince asked him.

"I thought it wiser at the moment," Lord Langford said, sitting down in one of the comfortable armchairs.

"What has happened? Please tell us what has happened," Yolisa asked breathlessly.

Lord Langford drank a little more wine from his glass before he replied,

"It was very wise and exceedingly clever of you, Your Royal Highness, to escape as you did. I gather from Ajax that it was only a matter of a few minutes before you saw the Russians entering the Palace."

"I knew that I was in danger," the Prince said quietly, "and Yolisa was aware of it at the same time. If she had not come to me and I had been obliged to arouse her as I expected to do, it would have been too late."

"That is what I understood," Lord Langford said. "I can only thank God that what Yolisa calls her *Third Eye* saved you both."

"We both saw the Russians going into the Palace when someone inside opened the door for them," Yolisa said and then added in a low voice to the Prince, so that her uncle could not hear her, "we were literally just — *one minute to love.*"

She smiled at her uncle and then asked him,

"What happened after that?"

"I understand that Your Royal Highness told Ajax to raise the guard immediately. They rushed in to find the Russians in your Private Apartments and killed them all."

Yolisa made a sound of horror but did not interrupt.

"It was then," Lord Langford went on, "that the troops on guard in the Palace took matters into their own hands."

"What happened?" the Prince asked.

"They went down into the City to rouse the rest of the Army and to tell the people what had happened," Lord Langford said and then paused.

Neither the Prince nor Yolisa spoke. They just listened intently with their eyes fixed on him.

"I don't think," he continued, "that until that moment the people of Kavalla realised how much they loved you or how important it was for them that you should be their Ruler and not the Russians."

"So what did they do?" the Prince enquired.

"They took it upon themselves with, of course, the help of the Army, to slaughter every Russian that they could lay their hands on."

He stopped for a moment to look at the Prince and then went on,

"Those who could ran for their lives. Some may have got across the border, but the majority were killed in the villages who rose, just as the City had, to destroy an enemy who had tried to deprive them of the Prince they loved."

"I must go back at once!" the Prince exclaimed.

Lord Langford shook his head.

"No! That would be a mistake, Your Royal Highness."

"Why?" the Prince asked. "If they are fighting for me, I must be with them and take command."

"At the moment there is far too much turmoil," Lord Langford replied. "You might easily be hit by a stray bullet or encounter a Russian who has not yet been discovered."

There was silence.

Then the Prince asked,

"What do you think I should do, my Lord?"

"Stay here until I am able to inform you that you can return triumphantly and rule your country without interference, at any rate for a short time."

He smiled before he added,

"At least until Her Majesty Queen Victoria supplies you with the protection of the Union Jack in the shape of an English Royal bride."

There was further silence as he finished speaking.

Then Yolisa said in a small rather frightened voice,

"We have — something to tell you — Uncle Harold."

"What is that?" Lord Langford replied, putting out his hand towards her.

Yolisa slipped her hand into his.

At the same time she looked at the Prince.

Somehow the words which she knew that she had to say would not come to her lips.

"What we have to tell you," the Prince said quietly, "is that Yolisa and I were married by Father Stavros as soon as we arrived here. We are very happy and we hope that you will not be angry at our taking such an important step. But for both of us it was simply inevitable."

Lord Langford stared at him.

"You were married here in the little Church?" he said. "Then, of course, it could be annulled."

"That will never happen," the Prince said. "I love Yolisa and she loves me. As you have been told, we have a joint awareness which is very different to what is felt by ordinary people. It is completely impossible for either of us to live our lives without the other."

Lord Langford took his hand from Yolisa's and put it up to his forehead.

"I don't know what to say," he said. "I can understand your feelings for each other and that they are very different from what is felt by ordinary men and women."

He paused before he went on more firmly,

"Equally if Kavalla does not have the protection it needs from England, the Russians will strive over and over again to destroy you, because, as we both know, the one thing they must achieve is access to the Mediterranean by any means."

"I know all that," the Prince said, rising to his feet and walking across to the window, "but Yolisa is my wife and I will never, under any circumstances, marry anyone else."

"I suppose," Lord Langford stated in a low voice, "it could be a Morganatic marriage."

"No!" the Prince asserted sharply. "If I return to sit on the Throne of Kavalla, Yolisa will sit beside me."

He spoke positively and his voice seemed to ring out in the small room.

Yolisa ran towards him and put her head against his shoulder.

"You have to think of your people, darling," she said. "Perhaps if I kept in the background no one would be aware that I was there."

The Prince smiled.

"You are far too lovely," he said, "for people not to notice you and then find it impossible to forget you."

He touched her forehead lovingly with his lips before he went on,

"And I want you with me, helping me and inspiring me both by day and by night."

She looked up at him and it was impossible for either of them to say any more.

The love in both their eyes and on their faces was very moving.

Lord Langford said almost beneath his breath,

"There must be something we can do."

"Surely," the Prince replied, "in Yolisa's long Family Tree such as all your countrymen appear to have, there is some ancestor of hers who is related to Royalty even if it is only distantly."

Yolisa gave a little laugh.

"Mama was a Stuart, but I doubt if the Queen would be impressed by that!"

To her astonishment Lord Langford sprang to his feet.

"A Stuart!" he exclaimed. "But, of course, the Stuarts provided Scotland with five Kings well before King James VI of Scotland became King James I of England."

"I remember Mama talking about it," Yolisa said.

"What is more important," Lord Langford continued as if she had not spoken, "Walter Stuart married Princess Marjory, daughter of Robert the Bruce, King of Scotland,

and from them descended the Royal House of Stuart."

"But I have always understood from Mama," Yolisa said, "that the Queen, because they are Catholic, will not accept the Stuarts or have anything to do with them."

Lord Langford smiled.

"You are out of date, my dearest," he said. "There are three Dukedoms held by the Stuarts and the Dukedom of Albany was bestowed on her fourth son, Prince Leopold, by his mother, Queen Victoria."

"Cannot that make things very different for us?" the Prince asked.

He looked at Lord Langford and added pleadingly,

"Surely, my Lord, if no one else can help us, you can."

"I promise Your Royal Highness I will do everything in my power and I just cannot think why I was so stupid as not to remember the Stuarts myself."

Lord Langford picked up his glass of wine, finished it and then said,

"Give me some more wine and something to eat quickly before I return to the City."

"What are you going to do?" Yolisa asked him.

"I am going to the British Embassy to put through a coded message to Queen Victoria and to the Prime Minister, the Marquis of Salisbury," Lord Langford said. "You must pray that the answer I hope to receive as soon as possible will be what we require."

Lord Langford spoke with the enthusiasm for his task that had made him so successful in everything he undertook.

He left the Prince and Yolisa about twenty minutes later taking one of their horses to ride back.

The horse he had ridden there would be tired and the quicker he reached the City the sooner he would be in touch with Her Majesty the Queen.

Yolisa kissed him goodbye.

"Thank you so much, Uncle Harold, for being so understanding," she said. "Nikos was sure that you would appreciate, where other people would not, what we mean to each other."

Lord Langford smiled.

"I have never seen two people look happier or more radiant," he said. "So please do pray that I shall bring you good news."

He rode away and Yolisa moved into the Prince's arms.

"How could you be so clever," she murmured, "as to make me remember the Royal Line of the Stuarts?"

"I think once again that it was the voice of God," the Prince replied. "So my darling, let's go into the Church and thank God for His inspiration and ask Him to make sure that we achieve what we want."

The Church was empty and they knelt and prayed at the altar.

As they did so, although her eyes were shut, Yolisa felt as if the light that had enveloped them at their marriage was streaming over them again.

She was sure that it was a sign from God that all would be well.

That she could be the wife of the Prince without leaving the country at risk from the Russians.

It was growing late the following day and the sun was sinking lower in the sky.

Yolisa looking through the window now said,

"There is someone approaching on horseback."

The Prince came immediately to her side and put his arm round her shoulders.

"Let's hope," he said, "that it's

your uncle."

"I am sure it is," Yolisa whispered.

It was a few minutes later before the rider she had seen in the distance canter through the trees towards them.

It was indeed Lord Langford.

Yolisa and the Prince knew before he dismounted that he had good news for them.

"You are back, Uncle Harold!" Yolisa exclaimed. "We did not really expect you until tomorrow or even later."

"I managed to speed up all the thinking and talking at Windsor Castle," Lord Langford laughed. "Which is a victory in itself!"

He dismounted.

One of the students came running

to take the horse from him to lead it to the stable.

They walked in silence into the house and only when they were in the sitting room did Yolisa burst out,

"Tell us, Uncle Harold, what has happened. I cannot wait politely to hear what you have achieved."

"What I have arranged," Lord Langford said, "is that you will be married in two days' time in the Cathedral and it will be an excitement that will take the Kavalleans' minds off recent events in the City."

"Married!" the Prince exclaimed. "But we are already married!"

"No one is to know that," Lord Langford said, "because it would spoil the happiness of those who saved you from the Russians and who are waiting fervently for your return to the Palace."

"And we can be married with the Blessing of Her Majesty the Queen?" the Prince asked.

Because it was such a vital question, Yolisa held her breath.

"Her Majesty has understood the importance of Kavalla coming immediately under the protection of the British Crown," Lord Langford declared solemnly. "She has therefore given her blessing for the marriage to take place between the reigning Prince and the Duchess of Steorn."

The Prince and Yolisa both stiffened as if turned to stone and stared at Lord Langford.

"The Duchess of Steorn?" Yolisa asked. "But whoever is she?"

"She is someone, my dearest, who has descended from the Royal Stuarts and whose Dukedom is now added to those of the Royal Dukes of Albany, Rothesay and Lennox."

The Prince gave a gasp and Lord Langford went on,

"There is no direct male heir, but as you know, being a Scot, in Scotland a woman can succeed to a Peerage. So you, my dearest niece, now become the Duchess of Steorn. I think, seeing who you are and with your Scottish blood, you should know what the name means in Gaelic."

Yolisa stared at him and then she said,

"Gaelic, but of course it means, 'to guide by the stars'."

Lord Langford gave a little laugh.

"Nothing could be more appropriate. Both of you have been guided by the stars and it is the stars which I know will guide you in the future and that you will protect Kavalla from ever falling into the hands of the Russians."

Yolisa gave a little cry and flung her arms around her uncle.

"Thank you, thank you, Uncle Harold!" she cried out. "How can we ever tell you how wonderful you are?"

"And I shall give you the highest award available in Kavalla," the Prince proclaimed, "but I think, my Lord, your real reward will really lie in the fact that you have made two people ecstatically happy."

Lord Langford put his hand on the Prince's shoulder.

"You and your country, Sire, are of great importance to the British Empire and I assure you that it will stand by you in the future."

"I just don't know — what to say," Yolisa said. "It is so wonderful and something I know that only you, Uncle Harold, could have achieved for us."

"Now we have to act very quickly," Lord Langford said. "It is absolutely essential that no one should know that you have been here together or, of course, that you are already married."

Yolisa's eyes widened.

"What do I have to do?" she asked a little anxiously.

"A British yacht which is owned by a friend of mine, whom I can trust with my own life and your reputation," Lord Langford said, "is at the moment anchored off-shore very near here."

He smiled at them both before he went on,

"You and I will go aboard at once, and we will arrive at Kavalla late on Friday evening, just in time for you to be fitted with the gown you will wear on Saturday when you are married in the Cathedral."

"Can everything possibly be ready in time?" the Prince asked.

"The Prime Minister has been working feverishly on the arrangements because he was confident that there would be no difficulty at gaining Queen Victoria's approval. And the whole City, having disposed of the Russians, will be preparing to give you the most exciting and joyful Wedding that anyone has ever known."

"I have always heard that you are a very fast worker, my Lord," the Prince said. "I feel now as if I am in an Express train which is breaking all records!"

"You will certainly feel like that in two days time," Lord Langford said, "and you must forgive me if I now take Yolisa away from you, just in case some nosey parker is a bit more intelligent than the rest and thinks of searching for you here.

They all know that you are in hiding and you can imagine that every citizen in the country wants to be the first to tell you the Russians have been driven out and will never again be accepted in Kavalla."

He gave them just five minutes to say goodbye to each other before he and Yolisa set off towards the sea.

It was not a long way, but it meant that they first had to travel through the woods and then over some open land before they reached the yacht.

The Prince had held her very close in his arms.

"I love you and adore you," he sighed, "and it is going to seem like a million years before you are close to me like this again."

"Then we never need to be parted again," Yolisa said. "Oh, my darling wonderful Nikos, how lucky we have been and how good God has been to us!"

"I shall stay with Father Stavros tonight," the Prince told her, "and talk to him of what we shall do in the future. I know that he has many ideas he wants put into action, which will be of great benefit to the country and how can we reject any of them considering what he has done for us?"

"I love you, I love you," Yolisa whispered. "And to be married to you will be — very exciting. But I think sometimes, when we have been working hard, we must come back here. Just to be alone — and bathe in our special pool where no one can see us."

"We will do that every year and each will be an extra honeymoon," the Prince said. "What is more, I intend to have another honeymoon shortly after our Wedding. But I expect we shall have to visit every town in the country first."

He kissed her before he added,

"Incidentally I want them to see what a beautiful bride I have."

"I want them to realise that I have the most brilliantly clever and handsome husband who ever existed," Yolisa replied firmly.

The Prince laughed and kissed her again.

Then, on Lord Langford's advice,

he stayed in the house while they walked away into the woods.

It was already nearly midnight three days later before the Prince and Princess of Kavalla said 'goodbye' to their last guests.

"It was just the most wonderful Wedding, Your Royal Highness, I have ever attended," one of the Councillors said, "and it is one the people of Kavalla will never forget."

"As my wife and I will never forget as well," the Prince said quietly.

It seemed impossible to Yolisa that so much had been done in so short a time.

The whole City had been decorated for the occasion and the flowers and flags were overwhelming.

From the moment Yolisa walked down the steps in the front of the Palace wearing one of the white gowns she had brought with her from England the cheering began.

The gown had a long train which had been extended by a team of seamstresses from the City and they had gone without sleep for two days and nights.

The Prime Minister had really risen to the occasion.

He had organised everything, which the Prince on his return had approved of as being spectacular and inspiring.

The Prince was driven first to the Cathedral in a gold coach drawn by white horses.

And Yolisa, escorted proudly by her uncle, Lord Langford, had followed in the glass coach so that everyone in the City could see her.

It had been the idea of the Prime Minister's wife that there should be ten small bridesmaids wearing white dresses to follow Yolisa up the aisle.

They carried pink bouquets and wore pink wreaths on their heads. They looked so sweet and so attractive that every mother in the Cathedral and in the Square who could see them was moved to tears.

The Marriage Service was then performed by the Archbishop of Kavalla assisted by six Priests.

There had been enough time to notify everyone of consequence in the country who should have a place reserved for them in the Cathedral.

The crowd of Kavalleans waiting outside was immense and they threw bouquets of flowers for the bride and bridegroom to walk on.

And they almost filled the open carriage they travelled in back to the Palace.

It made everyone forget how many dead Russians had strewn the streets only a few days earlier.

There followed a magnificent dinner party held in the vast Palace Banqueting Hall.

The huge crowd outside called for the bride and bridegroom again and again to appear on the steps.

The Prime Minister had ordered

fireworks which held the children enthralled and, when darkness came, they created flashes of brilliance in a sky which was already filled with many stars.

They were, Yolisa thought, part of the Fairytale which had been hers ever since she had come to Kavalla.

Now as she and Nikos walked upstairs she thought that no one could be more fortunate than she had been.

She could only pray that she would be able to help the people of the country to become as happy as she and the Prince were.

After a superb dinner and endless speeches they excused themselves and walked slowly up the stairs.

They reached the State bedroom

and Yolisa saw that it had been transformed.

There were flowers everywhere.

Flowers which scented the air and made the whole room a bower of beauty.

The heavy dark red curtains over the Royal bed had vanished and in their place were soft blue ones which made her think of the summer sky.

The furniture had been changed too.

Gilded tables which she had admired in other rooms had been moved in.

The heavier furniture, even though it was antique, had been replaced by what was light and beautiful.

"How could you have done all this so quickly?" Yolisa asked the Prince.

He knew what she meant and smiled at her.

"Everyone in the Palace wanted my bride to feel happy on her Wedding night," he said, "but they have no idea that she is clever enough to have had two!"

Yolisa laughed and put her finger up to his lips.

"Even the walls have ears," she said, "and no one must ever know."

"But I know," the Prince said, "and I am not going to wait another moment, my precious, to tell you how much I love you and how much I want you. It has been agony these last two days going to bed without you and waking to find myself alone. Now thank God I don't have to wait any longer."

As he was speaking, he came closer to Yolisa and was taking off her tiara.

It had replaced the crown he had placed on her head during the Wedding Service.

Now he was undoing the glittering white gown she was wearing.

As it fell to the ground, he held her against him.

Then, picking her up in his arms, he carried her to the large bed.

It was where the Rulers of Kavalla had slept for many generations.

Yolisa had told her lady's maids not to wait up for her, but she had not expected that the Prince would so readily take their place!

However, because she loved him, she was content to do anything he wished.

A few seconds later he slipped into bed beside her.

She turned towards him with a little cry of joy.

He had blown out the guttering candles and pulled back the curtains.

The moonlight was pouring in and turning the room into a Fairyland of silver and the stars were twinkling overhead in the sky.

All that Yolisa could think of was that the Prince was close to her again and his lips were on hers.

An ecstasy was rising within them both to carry them into the dream world where they were no longer two people but one.

Yolisa could feel the rapture moving within her.

She knew that Nikos's heart was beating as furiously as hers.

"I love you, God how I love you!" the Prince said in a deep voice. "You are mine, my darling, and we will never be parted again, never, never!"

Then he was kissing her again fiercely, possessively and passionately, as if he was afraid that he might lose her.

She could feel her whole body melting into his.

They were a part of each other.

The wonder of it was as perfect as the scent of the flowers and the magic of the moonlight.

"I love you, I adore you," Yolisa whispered.

As the Prince kissed her, she knew that he needed her as she needed him.

She prayed, as she had in the Cathedral, that she would give him plenty of sons and daughters who would love Kavalla and cherish their country.

She prayed too that they would keep Kavalla protected and safe from the Russians as it was now.

"You are mine," the Prince sighed. "Mine, my darling, and, although we have passed through so many difficulties to find each other, no one can separate us now."

"No one," Yolisa whispered. "God

has joined us from now to Eternity."

"And that is something we will never forget," the Prince said.

Then he was kissing her again.

All she could think of was the wonder of him and their sublime love for each other, which would last for Eternity and even beyond.

Outside the people of Kavalla watched the last fireworks explode in the sky and fall over the trees beneath them.

It seemed incredible to them that so much had happened so quickly.

They knew that in ridding themselves of the Russians who had menaced them they had achieved a great victory for their country.

It would be of great benefit not only to them and to their children but to their grandchildren as well.

Kavalla was safe.

Even the poorest and least important citizen was aware of that.

Great Britain, which was certainly the greatest country in the world, had blessed them with a British Queen.

The Union Jack would fly beside the Kavalla flag on all occasions.

Eventually the last of the merrymakers began to think that it was time to go home and the children in their mothers' arms were already asleep.

Everyone had enjoyed a Wedding that was so different from any they had known before.

They knew it meant not only security for Kavalla, but an era of prosperity that everyone would benefit from.

It was something that most of its people were intelligent enough to realise was essential to them and their future.

Otherwise they would succumb, as had so many Balkan States, to the menace of the Russian Army and the ambitions of the Russian Czar.

"We are safe now," the Prime Minister said with a note of satisfaction as he went up to bed.

"You must be feeling dead with all the work you have done," his wife responded, "to make this the very best Wedding I have ever attended."

The Prime Minister smiled.

"I admit to feeling my age, and a bit more," he replied, "but it is worth it. I have never seen two young people more in love with each other."

He gave a little laugh and went on,

"That is what we want in a country, not a Ruler and his wife who are figureheads, but two people who want to share their love with everyone else because they are so happy and so obviously content with each other."

He spoke with a feeling which for him was unusual and his wife looked at him in surprise.

"You sound as if you are envious,"

she said. "You know I love you, although I don't often say so."

"Well, there are two people who are saying it tonight with a great deal of fervour and undoubted sincerity," the Prime Minister replied. "It is something we might try for ourselves."

His wife laughed.

"And why not? If they can do it, we can do it too and don't tell me that you are too old."

"Of course I am *not!*" the Prime Minster asserted firmly.

He then kissed his wife in a way he had not done for a long time.

ABOUT THE AUTHOR

Barbara Cartland who sadly died in May 2000 at the age of nearly 99 was the world's most famous romantic novelist who wrote 723 books in her lifetime with worldwide sales of over 1 billion copies and her books were translated into 36 different languages.

As well as romantic novels, she wrote historical biographies, 6 autobiographies, theatrical plays, books of advice on life, love, vitamins and cookery. She also found time to be a political speaker and television and radio personality.

She wrote her first book at the age of 21 and this was called *Jigsaw.* It became an immediate bestseller and sold 100,000 copies in hardback and was translated into 6 different languages. She wrote continuously throughout her life, writing bestsellers for an astonishing 76 years. Her books have always been immensely popular in the United States, where in 1976 her current books were at numbers 1 & 2 in the B. Dalton bestsellers list, a feat never achieved before or since by any author.

Barbara Cartland became a legend in her own lifetime and will be best remembered for her wonderful romantic novels, so loved by her millions of readers throughout the world.

Her books will always be treasured for their moral message, her pure and innocent heroines, her good-looking and dashing heroes and above all her belief that the power of love is more important than anything else in everyone's life.

The employees of Thorndike Press hope you have enjoyed this Large Print book. All our Thorndike, Wheeler, and Kennebec Large Print titles are designed for easy reading, and all our books are made to last. Other Thorndike Press Large Print books are available at your library, through selected bookstores, or directly from us.

For information about titles, please call:
  (800) 223-1244

or visit our website at:
  gale.com/thorndike

To share your comments, please write:
  Publisher
  Thorndike Press
  10 Water St., Suite 310
  Waterville, ME 04901